WATCH & LEARN AMERICAN ENGLISH
with ANIMATED CHARACTERS

看動畫瘋美式英語

魔鏡魔鏡，救救我的Chinglish!

呂丹宜 Dannie Lu◎ 著

誰是世界上英語說最溜的人？

大主題【家庭親情】、【友情愛情】、【學校工作】、【生活娛樂】
量級閱讀48篇動畫故事！
情境對話：精選動畫人物的經典台詞，延伸情境對話，加速記憶聯想道地的美式英文語彙
單字解析：補充單字片語解析，擴充口說英文詞庫
換句話說：學習另一種活潑、新穎的說法，讓你的口語英文更自然

心看動畫電影，同步吸收美式英文！

MUST WATCH! MUST READ!

典收錄冰雪奇緣、怪獸大學、腦筋急轉彎、羅雷司、史瑞克、
人特攻隊、海底總動員、鯊魚黑幫等動畫經典台詞

MP3

動畫卡通，一直是我和孩子的共同親密經歷，陪伴孩子看動畫時，讓我們關係緊密，故事的角色與想傳達的理念、知識、英文字句，都豐富了我們的生命旅程。雖然孩子都大了，但我們對動畫卡通的熱情依然不減。撰寫這本書，讓我重新回味了以前和孩子走過的歲月，細細品味每一部動畫，仍是喜愛異常。

精心挑選的十部動畫，包括《海底總動員 Finding Nemo》、《鯊魚黑幫 Shark Tale》，這兩部開啟了孩子們對海底生物的了解，也學會尊重生命，愛惜海底生物；《羅雷司 The Lorax》，是少有探討環保，重視種樹及汙染的動畫；《怪獸大學 Monster University》鼓勵孩子們克服天生的不足，勇敢去追夢。《冰雪奇緣 Frozen》，讓孩子知道，每個人的天賦不同，要互相尊重，並善用自己的天賦，為人類造福；《腦筋急轉彎 Inside out》，更是一部適合大人觀看的電影，帶我們走進一場大腦醫學殿堂，以淺顯的卡通解釋艱澀的情緒醫學。

當然孩子的好英文，幾乎都是拜動畫電影所賜呢！在這機緣下，願以帶領自己孩子的經驗，帶領讀者一起進入動畫卡通英文學習的殿堂，再品味精心為您設計的內容，也期盼您的英文因動畫卡通的美好而蒸蒸日上。

呂丹宜 Dannie Lu

Editor
編者序

台灣學生一向熟悉的英文學習方式就是，翻開教科書、單字書或是參考書，開始從第一章節讀，辛苦地讀完了，能記在腦海裡的卻是有限，即使全記住了也不見得能夠好好活用。於是在跟外國人交流時，常常會出現一些溝通上的阻礙，舉凡,字詞誤用，或是文法等。

撇開教科書，其實還有許多有趣的方式與媒介可以學好英文。本書特地選取了迪士尼、皮克斯、夢工廠等動畫電影，如：冰雪奇緣 Frozen、腦筋急轉彎 Inside Out、羅雷司 The Lorax、史瑞克三世 Shrek the Third、海底總動員 Finding Nemo、鯊魚黑幫 Shark Tale、超人特攻隊 The Incredibles、怪獸大學 Monster University、食破天驚 1、2 Cloudy with a Chance of Meatballs I、II、北極特快車 Polar Express 等，藉由動畫人物的台詞，熟悉美語。

期許讀者邊享受動畫卡通電影的同時，也能一起學會電影中的口説英文。不僅訓練了聽力，也能因為動畫內容的牽引加深了英文學習上的記憶力。

編輯部

Contents
目次

2 Part 友情愛情

3 Part 學校工作

4 Part 生活娛樂

1
Part

家庭親情

Unit 1

冰雪奇緣
Don't Chuck Me Out.

動畫經典佳句

"So, we were so close. We could be like that again."
過去我們是這麼的親近,我們可以再像過去那樣。

"Please, don't chuck me out again. Please don't slam the door. You don't have to keep your destiny."
請不要再趕我出去,不要關上門,你不必再自己守著你的命運。

"For the first time and forever, we can fix this hand in hand. We can head down this mountain together."
這是第一次也是永遠,我們可以手牽手一起解決問題,一起走出這個險阻。

動畫內容敘述

Elsa, Princess of Arendelle, possesses cryokinetic powers, with which she is able to produce or manipulate ice, frost and snow at will. The royal couple isolates the children in the castle until Elsa learns to control her magical powers. Afraid of hurting her younger sister, Anna, Elsa spends most of her time being alone in her room; a rift develops between the sisters as they grow up. Elsa flees from the castle. She vows never to return and builds herself a solitary ice palace high in the nearby mountains. Meanwhile, Anna leaves Arendelle, sets out in search for her sister, determines to return her to Arendelle, ends the winter and mends their relationship.

艾莎，Arendelle 王國的公主，她擁有冷凍的力量，她可以任意製造或操控冰、霜及雪。國王及皇后將孩子們隔離，直到艾莎學會控制她的能力。害怕再傷害到她的妹妹安娜，艾莎絕大部分時間都自己一個人待在房內，漸漸地兩姊妹之間產生了隔閡。艾莎逃離了城堡，將自己封閉在鄰近山上的一座冰宮殿，且誓言不再回去。安娜離開王國，尋找姊姊，決定把她找回來，終止冬天，並修好她們的關係。

（參考網站：http://disney.wikia.com/wiki/Frozen）

 情境對話 Track 01

Bernice, Victor, Derek and Jack were good friends and co-workers. They used to hang out together. Jack is in some troubles recently. He found out the scandal of the whole business. He involved in a process of laundering money, but cannot get his way out of the difficult situation.

Jack: Stay away from me. You probably get hurt.

Bernice: No, we are trying to protect you.

Jack: You cannot do any help since the situation is too complicated.

Bernice: Please don't chuck us out and slam your door on us. It is not the end of the world.

Jack: You do not really understand. I am so afraid that you will get hurt.

Bernice: Trust us. You do not have to keep your destiny alone. We can help you face the problem hand in hand and head down this mountain with you. You don't have to live in fear. We will be right here. We love you.

▸▸ **中譯**

Bernice、Victor、Derek 和 Jack 是好朋友也是同事。他們過去經常一起消磨時間。現在，Jack 有了一些麻煩。他發現整個事業的醜聞。他被捲入洗錢的事件，卻無法讓自己脫身。

杰　克：遠離我，你可能會讓自己受到傷害。

柏妮絲：不，我們試著要保護你。

杰　克：你們幫不了忙，因為情況太複雜了。

柏妮絲：請不要趕我們出去，不要關上你的門。這並非世界末日。

杰　克：你不理解。我好害怕你們會受到傷害。

柏妮絲：相信我們。你不必自己孤獨地守著命運。我們可以幫助你面對問題，手牽手一起解決，陪你走出這個險阻。你不需要在恐懼中生活。我們將會一直在你身邊，因為我們都很愛你。

單字片語解析

close *adj.* 接近的

She is a close friend of our family.

她是我們家親密的朋友。

protect *v.* 保護

We should protect wildlife animals.

我們應該保護野生動物。

slam *v.* 猛地關上

The boy slams the door and breaks the window.

那個男孩猛的關上門並打破窗戶。

destiny *n.* 命運

She feels that it is her destiny never to return homeland.

她覺得她命中注定永遠無法再回到祖國。

chuck someone out *ph.* 趕某人出去

Don't chuck me out of your life.

不要把我趕出你的生命。

hand in hand *ph.* 攜手一起

We will conquer this problem hand in hand.

我們一起攜手克服這個困難。

你還可以這樣說

★ chuck someone out 把某人趕出去

也可以這麼說 drive someone out of

I drove Allen out of my sight.（我把艾倫趕出我的視線。）

★ show someone the door

He showed me the door.（他把我趕出去。）

★ kick someone out

We kick the man out of our house.（我們把那人趕出家門。）

★ hand in hand 攜手一起

也可以這麼說 together

We can work out this together.（我們可以一起解決問題。）

生活知識小補給

　　每一個人都有上天給予的天賦，這也讓你跟別人很不一樣。我們要先從接受自己，好好發揮這樣的天賦，不論是強的或是弱的能力，都是上天給予最好的禮物。像艾莎一樣，能好好發揮特殊能力；也像澳洲天生沒有四肢的力克胡哲，他的殘缺四肢，勵志故事，成了鼓勵人心最大的好模範。天生我材必有用，你的天賦是甚麼呢？

Part 1

Part 2

Part 3

Part 4

腦筋急轉彎

I Don't Speak Moron As Well As You.

動畫經典佳句

"I'd told you, you are too dumb to understand."

我已經告訴你，你實在太笨而無法理解。

"Of course your tiny brain is confused. Guess I'll just have to dumb it down to your level."

當然，你的小腦袋很疑惑。我猜我必須笨到像你一樣的程度。

"Sorry, I don't speak moron as well as you, but let me try. Duh!"

抱歉，我不能說笨話說得像你一樣好，但讓我試試。呆！

情境簡介

Like all of us, Riley is guided by her emotions-Joy, Fear, Anger, Disgust and Sadness. The emotions live in Headquarters, the control center inside Riley's mind, where they help advise her through everyday life. One day, Joy and Sadness leave the headquarters to find the missing core memory. Joy and Sadness come back to headquarters and are able to solve Riley's problem. As Joy and Sadness are stuck outside of the windows of headquarters, Disgust proceeds to make Angry get angry by insulting him in desperation, causing his head to explode with fire as he does when mad. The fire is used to melt the glass so Joy and Sadness could get into headquarters.

就像我們所有人一樣，萊莉為她的歡喜、憂傷、噁心、愉快及生氣的情緒所引導，他們住在她的大腦總部，在那裡幫助她面對每天的生活。有一天樂樂和憂憂離開總部去尋找萊莉遺失的核心記憶，她們尋得解法返回總部，卻卡在外頭的窗戶上。厭厭在情急之下，故意惹惱怒怒，讓他頭上噴火，熔掉玻璃，才讓憂憂及樂樂順利回到總部。

(參考網站：*http://disney.wikia.com/wiki/Inside_Out*)

1
Part

2
Part

3
Part

4
Part

 情境對話 Track 02

Warren has a very good temper. Nevertheless, he is often bullied in the school, which makes him upset all the time. His sister, Fanny, loves him so much. She tries to help him out while seeing him sobbing in the garden alone. Suddenly, an idea strikes on her. She approaches him...

Fanny: Hey, dude, did you fix up the problem you have with Ben?

Warren: Oh, well, I ...

Fanny: I'd told you, you are too dumb to understand.

Warren: It's not fair, I am just...

Fanny: Of course your tiny brain is confused. Guess I'll just have to dumb it down to your level.

Warren: How could you say so? You know I... and he...

Fanny: Sorry, I don't speak moron as well as you do, but let me try. Duh!

Warren: You really irritate me. I am not as weak as you think. Just get out of here!

Fanny: (chuckle) Well done, pal, let off your emotions. Just do like this. I am sure Ben will not make trouble again.

▶▶ 中譯

華倫脾氣很好。然而，這也讓他在學校常被霸凌，他很沮喪。他的姊姊芬妮很心疼他。她看到他獨自一人在花園啜泣，她很想幫他。突然，她有了一個想法。她走向他……

芬妮：嘿，老兄，你搞定和班的問題了沒？

華倫：喔，嗯，我……

芬妮：我已經告訴你，你實在太笨了，無法理解。

華倫：這不公平，我只是……

芬妮：當然你的小腦袋很疑惑。我猜我必須笨到像你一樣的程度。

華倫：你怎麼這樣講？你知道我……而且他……

芬妮：抱歉，我不能說笨話說得像你一樣好，但讓我試試。呆！

華倫：妳真的氣死我了，我不像妳想的這麼懦弱，滾開啦！

芬妮：（咯咯笑）做得好，老弟，把你的情緒發洩出來。就是這樣做。我相信班不會再惹麻煩了。

🔯 單字片語解析

🚩 **dumb** *adj.* 愚笨的

That was really a dumb decision.

那真是一個很笨的決定。

🚩 **tiny** *adj.* 微小的

Do not bother too much on these tiny matters.

別為這些小事太煩心。

🚩 **confuse** *v.* 困惑

His action confused me.

他的行為讓我很困惑。

🚩 **moron** *n.* 傻瓜

Jack is such a moron.

杰克真是一個傻瓜。

🚩 **as well as** *ph.* 和…一樣

He likes to watch TV as well as you.

他和你一樣喜歡看電視。

🚩 **duh** *int.* 笨

Duh! Everybody knows the sun comes out from the east.

笨！大家都知道太陽從東方出來的。

你還可以這樣說

★ too...to 太⋯而不能

也可以這麼說 so... that... not

The snow is so heavy that we cannot go to school today.

（雪下得太厚了，我們今天無法上學。）

★ as well as 和⋯一樣；不但⋯而且

也可以這麼說 not only... but also

Not only he but also you like to go fishing.（不只他而且你都喜歡釣魚。）

生活知識小補給

家人之間的拌嘴，有時也是感情升溫的方式，您相信嗎？京都大學研究團隊在京大研究猴子影像紀錄看到，猴子在發生衝突對峙之後，惹一方生氣的猴子會主動伸出手來緊抱一方，持續時間長達 8、9 秒鐘，還會大力搖擺身子，直到衝突化解為止。憤怒是一種情緒的發洩，也是彼此做更深入了解的一種方式。但不要忘記，事後可以學學猴子，給與對方大大的擁抱，感謝對方願意協助你宣洩情緒，讓你的身心靈達到更好的平衡！

Unit 3

羅雷司
It May Seem Small and Insignifiant.

"I know it may seem small and insignificant, but it's not about what it is. It's about what it can become."

我知道這可能好像又小又不起眼，但不是有關它是甚麼，而是它能夠成為甚麼。

"That's not just a seed, any more than you're just a boy."

這不是只是一顆種子，就像你不只是個男孩而已。

"Unless someone like you cares a whole awful lot, nothing is going to get better."

除非某人像你一樣非常關心，沒甚麼事會變得更好。

動畫內容敘述

Ted Wiggins, an idealistic 12-year-old boy, lives in "Thneed-Ville", a walled city that, aside from the citizens, is completely artificial. He sets out to find the one thing that will win him the affection of Audrey, the girl of his dreams, who wishes to see a real tree. Ted's energetic grandmother suggests he speak with the Once-ler on the matter, and he discovers that their city has been closed off from the outside world, which is a contaminated and empty wasteland. The Once-ler agrees to tell Ted about the trees if he listens to his story over multiple visits. Ted agrees, even after the mayor of Thneed-Ville, Mr. O'Hare, the greedy proprietor of a bottled oxygen company pressures him to stay in town.

泰迪，一個 12 歲愛空想的男孩，住在一個圍牆圍起來的城市絲尼鎮，除了市民，其他全是人工的。他出發去找一件可以贏得他夢中的女孩奧德莉的感情，她想看一棵真正的樹。泰迪那很有活力的奶奶建議他去找萬事樂談這件事，他發現他們的城市被封閉於外面的污染及荒廢的世界。萬事樂同意如果泰迪多來聽他的故事幾次，他就告訴泰迪有關樹的事。泰迪同意了，即使那個貪心的絲尼鎮氧氣瓶公司的擁有者歐海爾，強迫他留在城內。

(參考網站：https://en.wikipedia.org/wiki/The_Lorax_(film))

1 Part

2 Part

3 Part

4 Part

情境對話 Track 03

Ray is a 10-year-old boy. He cares about the environment in school. He notices a chemical factory near the school releases smog. The smog drifts to school in the afternoon every day. He tries hard to raise awareness in school, but seems in vain. He talks to his mum about his concern.

Ray: It seems nobody really cares.

Mum: I know it is hard. I do believe you are right.

Ray: I almost want to give up. Maybe I am wrong.

Mum: I know it may seem small and insignificant, but it's not about what it is. It's about what it can become.

Ray: I feel I am just an insignificant seed.

Mum: That's not just a seed, any more than you're just a boy.

Ray: I really have no idea what I should do to raise their awareness.

Mum: Unless someone like you cares a whole awful lot, nothing is going to get better.

Ray: Thanks mum. I know what I can do now. I need a group of friends with common consensus.

Mum: Excellent! Good boy.

▶▶ **中譯**

睿是個 10 歲男孩。他很關心學校的環境。他注意到學校附近的一家化學工廠釋放煙霧。煙霧每天下午會飄到學校。他很認真的在學校試圖引起大家對這件事的注意，但好像都是白費的。他跟媽媽談他的擔心。

睿 ：好像沒有人真的關心。

媽咪：我知道很難。我相信你是對的。

睿 ：我幾乎想要放棄了。可能我是錯的。

媽咪：我知道這可能好像又小又不起眼，但不是有關它是甚麼，而是它能夠成為甚麼。

睿 ：我覺得我只是一顆不起眼的種子。

媽咪：不是只是一顆種子，就像你不只是個男孩而已。

睿 ：我真的不知道我該如何做才能引起他們的注意。

媽咪：除非有人像你一樣非常關心，沒甚麼事會變得更好。

睿 ：謝謝媽咪。我現在知道我能做甚麼了。我需要一群擁有共識的朋友。

媽咪：太好了，好孩子。

1
Part

2
Part

3
Part

4
Part

單字片語解析

insignificant *adj.* 不起眼的

The problem is insignificant to her.

這些問題對她來說毫不重要。

seed *n.* 種子

Jack planted the magic seeds at the backyard.

杰克將魔法種子種在後院。

unless *conj.* 除非

You will not get the candies unless you finish the home-work.

除非你完成功課，不然你拿不到糖果。

你還可以這樣說

★ insignificant 無足輕重的

也可以這麼說 unimportant

It's ok. The missing parts are unimportant. （沒問題的，那遺失的零件是不重要的。）

★ meaningless

What happened last night is meaningless to her mother. （昨晚發生的事對她媽媽是毫無意義的。）

★ negligible

The money I donated is negligible.（我捐的錢是微不足道的。）

★ trivial

Even though it's trivial, you still have to pay attention.（即使它是微不足道的，你還是要注意。）

★ slight

Don't be so picky. The mistake he made is only slight.（不要這麼挑剔，他犯的錯只是一點點。）

生活知識小補給

　　羅雷司是一部探討環保的動畫卡通。大自然環境被人類破壞殆盡，我們享受許多文明帶來的產物，手機、電腦、服裝…等等，一旦它們成為垃圾，造成的災難也是非常巨大的。我們所穿的衣物，因為「快時尚」，每年約 85% 的衣物被丟棄，從 2013 年起，服裝已成為僅次於石化業，第二大汙染源了。平均每人每年約製造 31.5 公斤的衣物垃圾量。看到這一些數據，您想我們是否應該做一些甚麼呢？

Unit 4

史瑞克三世
Fall For Sb.'s Trick

動畫經典佳句

"And if he gives me trouble, I always have persuasion and reason."
如果他不甩我，我就講道理好好說服他。

"This really isn't up to you."
這件事由不得你。

"He will never fall for your trick."
他絕對不會被你打敗的。

 **動畫內容敘述**

King Harold, a frog, falls ill. His son-in-law, Shrek, and daughter, Princess Fiona are next in line to be King and Queen of Far Far Away. Shrek refuses and insists that an ogre as king is a bad idea. With his few breaths, the king tells Shrek that one other heir, his nephew Arthur, could be the new king. After the funeral, Shrek along with Donkey and Puss in Boots sets out to bring the new king back. As they are sailing off, Fiona runs to the dock and announces to Shrek that she is pregnant and he is going to be a father. Shrek begins to have nightmare about his future children on the journey to find Arthur.

哈洛德國王生病了。他的女婿史瑞克，及女兒費歐娜是遙遠王國的第一順位繼承人。史瑞克拒絕，並堅持一個怪物當國王是一個壞主意。最後幾口氣，國王告訴史瑞克，他的姪子亞瑟是另一位繼承人。葬禮之後，史瑞克和驢子及靴貓出發將新國王帶回。當他們啟航時，費歐娜跑到碼頭告訴史瑞克她懷孕的消息，而他即將成為父親。在旅途中，史瑞克想到他未來的孩子，噩夢連連。

（參考網站：https://en.wikipedia.org/wiki/Shrek_the_Third）

Part 1

Part 2

Part 3

Part 4

 情境對話 Track 04

On hearing the news that their son is planning to travel around the world after graduate from college, Stella and Jerry worry a lot. They discuss if it is possible to convince him to follow in Jerry's footsteps.

Jerry: Where does he think the money would come from?

Stella: He said he would be a street performer and make money out of it.

Jerry: He is too naive. How much can he make to be a street performer? He should do as I do and following my footsteps.

Stella: This really isn't up to you.

Jerry: If he gives me trouble, I always have persuasion and reason.

Stella: But, he is as stubborn as you.

Jerry: I will let him know how much effort he should make before pursuing his dream.

Stella: I do hope it works. Though I still think he will never fall for your trick.

Jerry: How about stop giving him pocket money and ask him to rely on himself from tomorrow?

Stella: Not a bad idea. Let's give it a shot.

▶▶ **中譯**

聽到他們兒子計畫在大學畢業後要環遊全世界，史黛拉和傑瑞很擔心。
他們在討論是否能說服他克紹箕裘，跟隨傑瑞工作。

傑　瑞：他覺得他錢要從那裡來呀？

史黛拉：他說他要做街頭藝人，然後賺錢旅遊。

傑　瑞：他太天真。做一個街頭藝人，他能賺多少？他應該做我做的
　　　　事，跟隨我的腳步走。

史黛拉：這件事由不得你。

傑　瑞：如果他不甩我，我就講道理好好說服他。

史黛拉：可是，他跟你一樣固執。

傑　瑞：我會讓他知道在追逐他的夢想之前，他該付出多少努力。

史黛拉：我真的希望說得動他。雖然我覺得他絕對不會被你打敗的。

傑　瑞：從明天開始我不再給他零用錢，讓他靠自己，如何？

史黛拉：不錯的主意，讓我們試試。

單字片語解析

⚐ **trouble** *n.* 麻煩

Her life is full of troubles.

她的人生充滿麻煩。

⚐ **persuasion** *n.* 說服

It is his persuasion that no insect should be allowed in the kitchen.

他堅信廚房不允許有任何昆蟲。

⚐ **reason** *n.* 理由

I have the reason to believe what she said.

我有理由相信她說的。

你還可以這樣說

★ fall for 迷戀

也可以這麼說 yearn madly for

Meggie yearns madly for the music played by Kennis. (美姬迷戀於肯尼斯彈奏的音樂。)

★ be infatuated with

Harry is infatuated with robot. (哈瑞迷戀機器人。)

★ be enamored of

Hans is enamored of planting orchids.（漢斯熱衷於種植蘭花。）

★ be gone on somebody

Kevin is gone on Vanessa.（凱文迷戀於薇尼莎。）

★ be hot on somebody

My cousin is hot on her classmate, Leon.（我表姊很迷戀她同學，里昂。）

★ take a fancy to

Julie takes a fancy to playing basketball.（茱莉非常衷情於打籃球。）

生活知識小補給

　　一個翻轉人生觀念的動畫電影，史瑞克。在傳統的故事裡，美麗的公主，嫁給英俊的王子，從此過著幸福快樂的神仙生活，然後王子繼承王位。這是一般人無法想望的人生。現實生活中又有多少對王子公主過著快樂人生？史瑞克，一個怪物，卻在意外中救了美麗的公主，他們沒有成為俊男美女，相反的，公主為愛祈求變成怪物。更神奇的是，史瑞克，努力不想成為國王，而追求一個平凡父親的角色。人生到底甚麼才是珍貴的？我想，史瑞克的故事，多少告訴了我們答案。

Unit 5

史瑞克三世
I Feel You, Dude.

動畫經典佳句

"I know you are busy not fitting in."
我知道你很忙不想被打擾。

"If you think this whole mad scene ain't dope, I feel you, dude."
如果你覺得這不是你的菜,我很了解你。

"I am doomed."
我完了。

動畫內容敘述

Prince Charming wants to kill Artie, because he believes he is the next king. In order to save Artie, Shrek tells Charming that Artie is just a fool to take his place as King. Charming believes Shrek and decides not to kill him. Artie, who has just developed trust on Shrek, is upset by this and runs away. Donkey and Puss are thrown into the tower with Fiona and the other ladies. Fiona is growing frustrated with the other princesses. Queen Lilian soon is fed up; she successfully smashed the stone wall of the prison. The women launch a rescue mission for Shrek, who is being captured. Donkey and Puss work to free Gingy, Pinocchio, the wolf and pigs and Dragon.

　　白馬王子要殺亞帝，因為他相信他是下一任國王。為了要救亞帝，史瑞克告訴白馬王子亞帝只是個笨蛋要搶他的王位。白馬王子相信史瑞克並決定不殺他。亞帝好不容易信任史瑞克，被這樣一說很沮喪，於是逃走。驢子和靴貓則與費歐娜及其他公主被丟進監獄裡。費歐娜對其他公主越來越失望。莉莉安王后很快就受不了，她成功地將監獄的牆打穿。這些公主開始進行拯救被抓起來的史瑞克的計劃。驢子和靴貓則去解救薑餅人、小木偶、大野狼、三隻小豬和龍。

（參考網站：https://en.wikipedia.org/wiki/Shrek_the_Third）

1 Part

2 Part

3 Part

4 Part

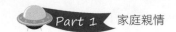 情境對話  Track 05

George was home alone. He was too bored on watching TV all day. He decided to play balls in the living room. Accidentally, his ball bounced to the antique vase of his parents. He was shocked. He tried to put the pieces together with glue the whole afternoon. His brother, Rick tries to help after he gets home.

Rick: I know you are busy not fitting in. What can I help with?

George: I am doomed.

Rick: How did it happen?

George: I was bored. I practiced a slam dunk and then...oops! The vase fell and shattered on the floor.

Rick: You are finished. It is mother's favorite.

George: I tried to fix it up the whole afternoon, but it is not working.

Rick: If you think this whole mad scene ain't dope, I feel you, dude.

George: What am I gonna do?

Rick: I would suggest you get advice from antique shops. The expert there knows better.

George: I don't know any.

Rick: Let's google it.

▸▸ 中譯

喬治一個人在家。他整天看電視太無聊了。他決定在客廳玩球。意外地,他的球彈到他父母的古董花瓶。他嚇壞了。整個下午他試著用黏著劑將碎片黏起來。他的哥哥,瑞克,回到家試著幫他。

瑞克:我知道你很忙,不想被打擾。我能幫甚麼忙嗎?

喬治:我完了。

瑞克:怎麼會這樣?

喬治:我太無聊。我在練灌籃,然後…慘了!花瓶掉下來碎了一地。

瑞克:你慘了。那是媽最喜歡的。

喬治:我整個下午試著要修好它,但是沒用。

瑞克:如果你覺得這整件事不是你預想的,我很了解。老兄。

喬治:我該怎麼辦?

瑞克:我建議你到古董店問問,那裡的專家可以給你好建議。

喬治:我不知道任何店。

瑞克:讓我們上網搜尋一下。

單字片語解析

doom *n.* 厄運

The tyrant met his doom after 2 years of domination.

那暴君統治了 2 年終於遭到厄運。

fit *v.* 適合

I quit my job because I don't think I fit the system.

我辭職了，因為我不認為我適合這個體系。

scene *n.* 一場（戲劇）

The whole scene of this play is marvelous.

這齣戲劇的場景真是不可思議。

你還可以這樣說

★ fit in 適合

也可以這麼說 adapt to

Marvin can adapt to this boarding house.（馬文對這住宿家庭很能適應。）

★ belong to

Jay does not belong to this group.（杰不屬於這個團體。）

★ dude 老兄

也可以這麼說 bro

It is pretty cool, isn't it, bro?（這很讚，不是嗎，老兄？）

★ buddy

Come on, buddy.（少來，老兄。）

★ homie

Lyle is my homie.（萊爾是我的好夥伴。）

生活知識小補給

面對一個極大的誘惑，你是否能不為所動？史瑞克被授權繼任王位，他，堅持一個怪物不能繼任王位。是他的信心不足嗎？部分原因，應該是的，他對自己醜陋的外表，沒有信心。而他對自己要追求的家庭與平凡生活，卻不遺餘力。觀今社會，有多少對自己沒有多少信心的人，卻張牙舞爪的謀取大位，最後坐上大位，處處展現無能，最後貪腐亂紀收場。讓筆者讚嘆，了解自己，不對富貴榮華所誘惑真是難能可貴呀！

Unit 6

北極特快車
Bring Up

動畫經典佳句

"Put him on the check-twice list for next year."
明年將他列入觀察名單。

"These poor toys have suffered enough being left to rust and decay in the back alleys and vacant lots of the world."
這些可憐的玩具，被人糟蹋夠了，就被扔在空蕩的角落裡，等著腐爛生鏽。

"What exactly is your persuasion on the big man? Since you brought him up."
那你心裡，對那個傢伙，又是怎麼想的？既然是你養育他長大的。

🛸 動畫內容敘述

On Christmas Eve, a boy witnesses a train called the Polar Express that is about to depart for the North Pole. The boy suspects when the conductor invites him. He finally decides to board the train. On the journey, they experience a lot of mysterious and risk events. During the trip, the conductor takes the two kids to a room with abandoned toys. They feel so sorry for those toys. A hobo scares the hero boy with an Ebenezer Scrooge puppet, and the boy retreats to the observation car where the girl and Billy are singing.

在聖誕夜前夕，一個男孩親眼見到一列北極特快車，要出發到北極去。當列車長邀請他時他很懷疑。他最後決定上車。在旅程中，他們經歷很多神秘且危險的事情。在旅途中，列車長帶兩個孩子到一間充滿廢棄玩具的車廂。他們為這些玩具感到難過。一個流浪漢用木偶嚇這個男孩，男孩嚇倒退到觀察車廂，那裡有個女孩和比利正在唱一首好聽的歌。

（參考網站：*https://en.wikipedia.org/wiki/The_Polar_Express_(film)*）

 情境對話 Track 06

Dad and Mum are discussing the gift they will prepare for their only son, Martin this Christmas. However, Dad seems a little reluctant to prepare the gift. Mum is a little worried that will let Martin down.

Mum: What's the gift we are going to prepare for Martin this year?

Dad: It's hard. Could we just leave it?

Mum: But, it's Christmas.

Dad: These poor toys have suffered enough being left to rust and decay in the back alleys and vacant lots of the world.

Mum: He is merely a child.

Dad: He is 10 years old. What exactly is your persuasion on the big boy? Since you brought him up.

Mum: Ok, I'll tell him to pack up and take good care of those toys he received in the past ten years.

Dad: Put him on the check-twice list for next year.

Mum: Sure. By the way, what's the gift in your mind? Let's get him a bicycle...

Dad: I would buy him a book instead of toys.

Mum: That sounds pretty good. Thank you, honey.

▶▶ **中譯**

爸爸和媽媽在討論今年聖誕節,要給他們的唯一兒子馬丁甚麼禮物。可是,爸爸似乎不大情願再給禮物,媽媽擔心那會讓馬丁失望。

媽媽:我們今年應該幫馬丁準備甚麼禮物呀?

爸爸:好難喔。可不可以不要談呀!

媽媽:可是,聖誕節耶!

爸爸:這些可憐的玩具,被人糟蹋夠了,就被扔在空蕩的角落裡,等著腐爛生鏽。

媽媽:他只是個孩子。

爸爸:他 10 歲了。那你心裡,對那個大孩子,又是怎麼想的?既然是你把他帶大的。

媽媽:好,我會告訴他要他打包並好好照顧他過去 10 年所收到的禮物。

爸爸:明年將他列入觀察名單。

媽媽:好。但是,你心裡有想甚麼禮物嗎?讓我們買一台腳踏車……

爸爸:我會買一本書給他,而不送玩具了。

媽媽:聽起來不錯,謝謝你,親愛的。

單字片語解析

🚩 **suffer** *v.* 遭受

The man suffered from cancer which caused a great pain.

那人遭受了癌症的巨大痛苦。

🚩 **rust** *v.* 生鏽

Rain rusts iron easily.

雨很容易使鐵生鏽。

🚩 **decay** *v.* 使腐爛

Strawberries decayed after the frost.

結霜後草莓都腐爛了。

你還可以這樣說

★ brought up 養育

也可以這麼說 raise

The boy was raised in orphanage. （那男孩在孤兒院長大的。）

★ nurture

The puppy is nurtured by its owner. （那個小狗被主人養大。）

★ suffer 遭受

也可以這麼說 experience

John had experienced the loss of beloved one. （約翰經歷過失去摯愛的痛。）

★ endure

I cannot endure her unreasonable request anymore.（我無法再忍受她無理的要求了。）

★ undergo

He needs to undergo his own destiny.（他需要去承受自己的命運。）

★ tolerate

You don't have to tolerate the critical review.（你不必忍受這樣嚴苛的批評。）

生活知識小補給

　　每年上萬噸的棄置玩具，造成環境上的汙染已不容忽視。許多藝術家紛紛將棄置玩具加上巧思，創造出玩具的第二春。現在很多機構設置二手玩具的交換平台，政府也開始設置嬰幼兒物資交換中心，為我們的地球盡一份心力。玩具總動員的卡通，也希望大家不要隨處棄置玩具，改變觀念。您家中是否有多餘的玩具？何不讓它們有更大的用途，讓我們一起珍愛地球吧！

1 Part

2 Part

3 Part

4 Part

Unit 7

鯊魚黑幫

It's A Sure Thing Guaranteed Cash Extravaganza.

動畫經典佳句

"Please just gimme some time."
請給我一 點時間。

"Don't make the same mistake that I did. I didn't know what I had until I lost it."
別犯跟我一樣的錯。我不知我擁有甚麼，一直到我失去它。

"It's a sure thing guaranteed cash extravaganza."
這絕對是付錢少，成本低，回收快的主意。

動畫內容敘述

An underachieving cleaner wrasse, named Oscar, dreams about being rich and famous while making his way to work as a tongue scrubber at a local Whale Wash. That is a job in which he follows his father's footsteps in the reef. Soon after arriving, he is called to the office by his boss, a pufferfish named Sykes, to discuss the fact that he owes "five thousand clams" and has to pay it back by the next day. After explaining this to his best angel fish friend Angie, she offers him a chance to pay back the money by pawning a pink pearl which was a gift from her grandmother.

一個在珊瑚礁繼承父親的工作，卻表現不佳的隆頭魚科清潔工，奧斯卡，在前往當地一家鯨魚清潔公司為鯨魚刮舌苔的路上，夢想變得有名又有錢。到達公司之後，他被他的河豚老闆史凱子，叫到辦公室，要他在第二天歸還他欠下的「5000 貝殼」。在告訴他的天使魚好友安姬後，安姬把她祖母送的一顆粉紅珍珠給他典當還錢。

(參考網站：https://en.wikipedia.org/wiki/Shark_Tale)

Part 1

Part 2

Part 3

Part 4

情境對話 🎧 Track 07

Kyle is crazy about lottery. He often dreams that he will be the winner. The jackpot for this term is one billion dollars. He tries to convince his father to combine the stakes.

Father: Wadaya doing here?

Kyle: Please gimme some time. Can you gimme some suggestions? I need numbers.

Father: Don't indulge yourself in the lottery that much.

Kyle: Look at this news, The jackpot this term is one billion dollars. Wow! I could be the one.

Father: Don't think too much.

Kyle: Let's combine our stakes together. I am sure we are gonna get more chances. It's a sure thing guaranteed cash extravaganza.

Father: You know why your mother left us?

Kyle: Why do you mention this?

Father: Don't make the same mistake that I did. I didn't know what I had until I lost it.

Kyle: You were a gambler?

Father: I finally realize the chance of winning is one in a billion. One thing for sure is that I can never win your mother back.

▸▸ **中譯**

凱爾熱衷於樂透。他常夢想他就是得獎者。這一期累積彩金是 10 億元。他想要說服他的父親一起下注。

爸爸：你在這裡做甚麼？

凱爾：請給我一點時間。你可以給我一些建議嗎？我需要數字。

爸爸：別太沉溺於樂透。

凱爾：看這個新聞，這一期累積彩金是 10 億元耶。哇！我可能就是那個幸運兒。

爸爸：別想太多。

凱爾：我們一起下注吧！我相信我們一定可以有更多機會中獎。這絕對是付錢少，成本低，回收快的生意。

爸爸：你知道你媽為何離開我們嗎？

凱爾：你為何提起這事？

爸爸：別犯跟我一樣的錯。我不知我擁有甚麼，一直到我失去它。

凱爾：你是個賭徒？

爸爸：我最後了解到贏錢的機會是 10 億分之一。但我確認我永遠贏不回你媽。

單字片語解析

gimme（縮寫）give me 給我

Please gimme the data you collected.

請給我你蒐集的資料。

mistake *n.* 錯誤

He promises that he will not make any mistake anymore.

他承諾他將不再犯錯。

lost *v.* 遺失的（過去式）

The boy lost his favorite toy.

那男孩遺失他最喜歡的玩具。

你還可以這樣說

★ sure thing 必然成功之事；毫無疑問的事

也可以這樣說 certainty

The victory of the team is a certainty.（這個團隊的勝利是無庸置疑的。）

★ guarantee 保證

也可以這樣說 ensure

This remedy can ensure you to soothe your pain.（這個療法可以保證減緩你的疼痛。）

★ promise

I cannot promise you to hand in the work tomorrow.（我無法跟你保證明天交出作業。）

★ give one's word

Johnson gives his word to his people.（詹森對他的人民許了一個承諾。）

生活知識小補給

你有甚麼夢想呢？要圓一個夢，不是一件容易的事。在生命中就有許多無法預期的事，阻擋在你面前，你可以勇敢突破難關達成夢想嗎？有人曾經將麗滋(Lizzie Velasquez)的 2 分鐘影片放到網站，並標上「世上最醜女人」的標題，許多人留言，請她幫忙將槍放她自己頭上，殺了她自己以謝世。她，得了罕見疾病，卻敞開心胸接受那些因她的病而霸凌她的人，並藉此讓自己善用這些負面影響讓自己成為一位激勵人心的演說家、作家。

Unit 8

鯊魚黑幫
You Never Take Sides Against The Family.

"If you sneeze, you don't wipe that boogie without my ok. Ok?"

如果你打噴嚏,沒有我的許可,不准擦掉鼻涕。懂嗎?

"Get your butts home. I'll tell your mom y'all doin' bad stuff."

滾回家。我會告訴你媽你做的壞事。

"You never take sides against the family. Ever."

你永遠不准背叛家人,永遠。

動畫內容敘述

A family of criminally-inclined great white sharks has a problem with one of their sons, Lenny, who is a vegetarian and refuses to act the part of a killer, wishing not to have to live up to those expectations in the wreck of the R.M.S Titanic. His crime lord father, Don Edward Lino, orders Lenny's more savage older brother Frankie to tutor Lenny in the family business. After the two sharks depart their father, Frankie sees Oscar being electrocuted by Sykes' two jellyfish enforcers Ernie and Bernie and sends Lenny off to attack. Accidentally, Frankie ends up by an anchor.

在失事的鐵達尼號船艙內，有犯罪傾向的大白鯊家族有一個兒子連尼有問題。他是個素食主義者，拒絕殺魚，而且希望不要在這樣的被期待下生活。他的黑幫老大父親，湯大尾，命令連尼比較兇殘的哥哥法蘭奇教連尼家族企業。當兩兄弟告別父親後，法蘭奇看到奧斯卡被史凱子的兩個水母部下恩尼及伯尼施以電刑，決定送連尼去攻擊他們。意外地，法蘭奇被一個錨給殺死。

（參考網站：https://en.wikipedia.org/wiki/Shark_Tale）

1 Part

2 Part

3 Part

4 Part

 情境對話 Track 08

Leo is a powerful wise man in the village. He heard that Ted from Bernice family is a bully. The villagers and his parents get headache about him. They submit a petition asking Leo to give him a lesson. Ted, a 15-year-old boy, is a little afraid of this powerful old man.

Leo: How do you survive after you quit school?

Ted: I steal from my parents.

Leo: Why don't you find a job?

Ted: No one wanna hire me.

Leo: You are such a trouble maker! You gotta go back to school, understand? If you sneeze, you don't wipe that boogie without my ok. Ok?

Ted: I cannot afford tuition fee.

Leo: I will pay for you. I will talk to the principal and get you back to school.

Ted: I...

Leo: No more words. Get your butt home. I'll tell your mom y'all doin' bad stuff.

(Ted is about to leave)

Leo: By the way, never take sides against the family. Ever. If I hear you make trouble to others or steal money again, you will definitely learn the consequence. Got me?

▶▶ 中譯

里歐是村落裡有權勢的智者。他聽說伯尼斯家的泰德是個惡霸。村民及他父母對他都很頭痛。他們請求里歐教訓他。泰德，一個 15 歲男孩，有點害怕這位有權勢的老人。

里歐：你休學後怎麼過活？

泰德：我從爸媽那裏偷錢。

里歐：你為什麼不找一個工作？

泰德：沒有人要雇我。

里歐：你真是個麻煩。你一定要回學校，知道嗎？如果你打噴嚏，沒有
　　　我的許可，不准擦掉鼻涕。懂嗎？

泰德：我付不起學費。

里歐：我幫你付。我會跟校長講，讓你回學校去。

泰德：我……

里歐：別再說了。滾回家。我會告訴你媽，你做的壞事。
　　　（泰德準備要離開）

里歐：還有，永遠不准背叛家人，永遠。如果我再聽到你惹麻煩或再偷
　　　錢，你就要自負後果，聽到沒？

單字片語解析

sneeze *v.* 打噴嚏

Jack sneezed a lot after walking in the rain.

傑克淋了雨後一直打噴嚏。

wipe *v.* 擦

Wipe the window before you leave the house.

在你離開房子前擦窗戶。

boogie *n.* 一把鼻涕

The nanny wiped the boogie on the boy's face.

那保母擦去那男孩臉上的鼻涕。

你還可以這樣說

★ take sides 偏袒

也可以這樣說 be partial to

Our teacher is partial to boys.（我們老師偏袒男生。）

★ show undue

Don't show undue to your children.（不要偏袒你的孩子們。）

★ favor

I favor English literature than the other subjects.（比起其他科目我比較喜歡英國文學。）

★ side

Kelly sided against her mother's suggestion.（凱莉反抗媽媽的建議。）

🦋 生活知識小補給

　　聯合國糧農組織發表報告指出，全球 10 億 5000 萬頭牛所排放的二氧化碳，佔全球總排放量的 18%，不但比其他羊、雞、豬等家畜動物高出許多，更超越人類交通工具如汽車、飛機等。牛群的屁和排泄物會排出 100 多種污染氣體，其中氨的排放量就佔全球總量的 2/3，而氨正是導致酸雨的原因；甲烷排放量佔全球總量 1/3，這種氣體暖化地球的速度比二氧化碳快 20 倍。許多人為了保護環境，紛紛成為不只是個 vegetarian 素食者，而成為奶蛋素的 vegan 呢！

Unit 9

海底總動員
You Can't Hold On to Them Forever.

"I'm sorry. I don't mean to interrupt things."
對不起，我不是故意要打擾的。

"I promised him I'd never let anything happen to him."
我承諾他我不會讓任何事發生在他身上。

"He says it's time to let go. You can't hold on to them forever, can you?"
他說是時候放手了，你無法永遠抓住他們，不是嗎？

動畫內容敘述

In the Great Barrier Reef, two clownfish, Marlin and his wife Coral admire their new home and their clutch of eggs. Marlin was knocking unconscious when a barracuda attacks. He wakes up to find that Coral and all, but only one of the eggs left. Marlin names this last egg Nemo, a name that Coral liked. Marlin is a fretful and apprehensive father clownfish. He is very protective of his only child, Nemo. Nemo develops a smaller right fin as a result of damage to his egg during the attack, which limits his swimming ability. Worried about Nemo's safety, Marlin embarrasses Nemo during a school field trip.

在大堡礁，兩個小丑魚，馬林和他的妻子珊瑚，喜愛他們的新家及一窩小魚蛋。但當遭過一隻梭魚的攻擊時，馬林被撞到昏倒。他醒來時，發現珊瑚及所有蛋都不見了，只剩下一顆蛋。馬林將這個小魚取名為珊瑚喜歡的名字，尼莫。馬林是個恐懼焦躁的父親。他對唯一的孩子，尼莫，非常保護。尼莫有一個很小的鰭，因為當時梭魚的攻擊而受了傷，也限制了他游泳的能力。擔心尼莫的安全，馬林在學校的校外教學時令尼莫難堪。

（參考網站：http://disney.wikia.com/wiki/Finding_Nemo）

 Track 09

Kelly is an over protective mom. She worries a lot about her son, Kevin. It will be the first day for Kevin to go to a kindergarten the next day. Kelly is a little bit anxious. She is wandering around the house but does nothing. Larry, her husband notices that she is a little bit irritated.

Larry: I'm sorry. I don't mean to interrupt things. Are you OK?

Kelly: Kevin will go to school tomorrow. I worry that he cannot adapt himself in the school.

Larry: He has grown up. I am sure he will be ok. The teachers there are very nice, aren't they?

Kelly: I promised him I'd never let anything happen to him.

Larry: Nothing is gonna happen. He needs to explore his life. You cannot always keep him, or he will hate you in the future.

Kelly: I guess I'm worrying too much.

Larry: It's time to let go. You can't hold on to him forever, can you?

Kelly: Thank you, honey. I'll try to relax.

▶▶ 中譯

凱莉是個過度保護的媽媽，她很擔心她的兒子，凱文。隔天將是凱文第一天上幼稚園。凱莉有一些焦躁，她一直在家裡閒晃也沒做任何事。賴瑞，她的丈夫注意到她的不安。

賴瑞：對不起，我不是故意要打擾的。你還好嗎？

凱莉：凱文明天要上學。我很擔心他適應不了學校。

賴瑞：他已經長大了。我相信他可以的。那邊的老師很好呀，不是嗎？

凱莉：我承諾他我不會讓任何事發生在他身上。

賴瑞：沒甚麼事會發生的。他需要探索他的人生。你無法永遠留住他，否則以後他會很討厭你的。

凱莉：我猜我過度擔憂了。

賴瑞：是時候放手了，你無法永遠抓住他，不是嗎？

凱莉：謝謝你，親愛的，我會試著放鬆的。

單字片語解析

mean *v.* 用意

I don't mean to hurt.

我沒有傷害的意思。

interrupt *v.* 打斷

Mum doesn't like to be interrupted during her work.

媽媽不喜歡在工作中被打斷。

promise *v.* 承諾

Can you keep your promise?

你可以遵守承諾嗎？

你還可以這樣說

★ hold on 繼續；保持；堅持

也可以這麼説 carry on

We need to carry on reaching our goal.（我們需要堅持達到目標。）

★ keep up

The basketball coach requests us to keep up practicing to perfect.（籃球教練要求我們繼續練到完美。）

★ persist in

The marathon runners persist in reaching the finish line.（馬拉松選手堅持跑到終點。）

★ stand on

Could you just stand on a little longer?（你可以再堅持長一點時間嗎？）

生活知識小補給

　　澳洲大堡礁是世界最大的珊瑚礁岩，由 2,900 個個別礁岩及 900 座島嶼延伸超過 2,300 公里，面積高達 344,400 平方公里，座落在澳洲昆士蘭州的外海。在外太空可以見到由單一有機生命體組成的最大的結構。這個礁岩由幾十億的微小生物珊瑚蟲所組成，它支持著巨大的多元生物，並在 1981 年被列為世界遺跡。CNN 則將之列為世界七大奇蹟(seven natural wonders of the world)之一呢！

Unit 10

海底總動員
First-timer

動畫經典佳句

"You got serious thrill issues, dude."
你喜歡找特別的，老兄。

"You are doing pretty well for a first-timer."
對第一次新手而言，你做得很好。

"An entire ecosystem contained in one infinitesimal speck."
整個生態系統包含在一個微粒中。

動畫內容敘述

Marlin is worried about Nemo's swimming ability due to his abnormally small right fin which Nemo considers it to be his lucky fin. Nemo is sent to school but elopes on the first day thereby touching the bottom of a boat. This starts an argument between the father and son. Eventually, Nemo sneaks away from the reef and is captured by scuba divers. As the boat departs, a diver accidentally knocks his diving mask overboard. While attempting to save Nemo, Marlin meets Dory, a good-hearted and optimistic Regal Blue Tang with short-term memory loss. Marlin and Dory meet three sharks– Bruce, Anchor and Chum– who claim to be vegetarians.

馬林因為尼莫受傷的右鰭，尼莫稱之為幸運鰭，而擔心他的游泳能力。尼莫被送上學的第一天去碰觸了船的底部。這讓父子產生爭吵。最後尼莫偷跑，並被一位潛水伕捕獲。當船駛離開，一個潛水夫不小心將潛水夫蛙鏡掉到海裡。馬林試圖要去救尼莫，路上遇見一隻好心腸、樂觀但有短暫失憶的藍唐王魚多莉。馬林和多莉遇見三隻鯊魚；布魯斯、安哥和瓊，他們宣示要成為素食者。

（參考網站：*http://disney.wikia.com/wiki/Finding_Nemo*）

 情境對話  Track 10

Brook found a board game at the attic. The board game looks very fascinating. Nevertheless, he needs someone to play with. He sees his brother, Gail, is playing computer games. He invites Gail to play with him.

Brook: Gail, look at this. I found a treasure.

Gail: You got serious thrill issues, dude.

Brook: Ok, all new explorers must answer a science question.

Gail: Did so-call "killer bees" originate in Asia, Africa or South America?

Brook: Let me think. Um...Africa.

Gail: Correct.

Brook: My turn. Does a flower's stamen produce seeds, nectar or pollen?

Gail: I guess it's nectar.

Brook: No, sorry. It's pollen.

Gail: You are doing pretty well for a first-timer.

Brook: Thanks, mate. Name an ecosystem in one single item.

Gail: An entire ecosystem contained in one infinitesimal speck.

Brook: Cool, mate. Amazing!

Gail: An ecosystem doesn't have to be very large. My science teacher said so.

Brook: Let's move on...

▸▸ 中譯

布魯克在閣樓發現了一個桌上遊戲，看起來很好玩。但，他需要有人一起玩。他看到哥哥蓋爾正在玩電動。他邀請蓋爾跟他一起玩。

布魯克：蓋爾，看，我挖到寶了。

蓋　爾：你喜歡找特別的，老兄。

布魯克：好吧。所有的新探險家需要回答一個科學問題。

蓋　爾：所謂的「殺人蜂」來自亞洲、非洲還是南美洲？

布魯克：我想想，嗯……非洲。

蓋　爾：正確。

布魯克：輪到我。雄蕊製造種子、花蜜還是花粉？

蓋　爾：我猜是花蜜。

布魯克：喔，不對。是花粉。

蓋　爾：對第一次新手而言，你很行喔。

布魯克：謝啦，老兄。說出一個單一物品中的生態系統。

蓋　爾：整個生態系統包含在一個微小東西。

布魯克：很讚喔，老兄。真的很驚奇！

蓋　爾：一個生態系統不必一定要很大，我的科學老師說的。

布魯克：讓我們繼續……

1
Part

2
Part

3
Part

4
Part

單字片語解析

thrill *adj.* 可怕的

I prefer thrill movie than drama.

跟劇情片比起來，我比較喜歡恐怖電影。

issue *n.* 問題

Global warming has become a serious issue worldwide.

全球暖化成為世界的一個嚴重問題。

explorer *n.* 探險家

Indiana Jones was a famous explorer.

印第安那瓊斯是個著名的探險家。

你還可以這樣說

★ first-timer 新手

也可以這麼説 new hand

The company trains new hands intensively.（公司加強訓練新手。）

★ greenhorn

The mentor system is to help greenhorn.（曼托是幫助新手適應的系統。）

★ green hand

Fanny is assigned to help green hand in the company.（芬妮被公司指派負責幫助新手。）

★ beginner

Everybody has the experience of being a beginner.（每一個人都有當過新手的經驗。）

★ tenderfoot

The tenderfoot cannot adapt himself well here.（那個新手無法在這裡適應得很好。）

生活知識小補給

　　小丑魚住在鹽水的大海中，它們非常亮麗，有三條白色條紋在頭部、中間及尾巴，身長約 5-10 公分，雄魚比雌魚小。小丑魚有很多不同顏色，從藍色到黃色都有。他們與一些特種海葵共生，它們是唯一能與海葵共生而不被觸角螫昏的魚。它們很活躍，極具攻擊性。它們吃海葵吃剩的東西，包括浮游生物。它們生命之所以受到最大的威脅是因為人類，常被人類餵養在魚缸中，放了不對的海葵品種，因而將它們本來 6-10 年的壽命縮短到只剩 3-5 年。

Unit 11

超人特攻隊
Dish Out

動畫經典佳句

"Girl, I don't want to know about your mild-mannered alter ego."
女孩，我不想知道妳溫良恭謹的內在。

"There are a lot of leftovers that you can reheat."
那有很多剩菜可以加熱。

"I can totally handle anything this baby can dish out."
我可以完全處理任何這個孩子能搞出的事。

🛸 動畫內容敘述

Human gifted with super powers, were once seen as heroes. After facing several lawsuits over peripheral damages caused by their various good deeds, the government forces them into civilian relocation program and not to use their superpowers in exchange for anonymity. Bob and Helen Parr are supers, formerly known as Mr. Incredible and Elastigirl. Bob has unparalleled strength and Helen is able to stretch a long distance to reach places others can't. They have three children Violet, Dash, and Jack-Jack live as a suburban family in Metroville for fifteen years. Bob is dissatisfied with suburban life and his white-collar job and longs for the glory days. On some nights, Bob and his old friend Lucius Best– formerly known as Frozone–fight street crime, without acknowledging their wives.

有超能力的人，一度被認為是英雄。但在面對幾次的法院案件，因為他們的救人行徑所造成的破壞後，政府施行一個重置計畫，強迫他們回歸常人，隱姓埋名。鮑勃帕爾和海倫夫婦是超人，眾所周知的超能先生和彈力女超人。鮑勃有很大的力氣，而海倫能伸展得非常遠。他們有三個孩子小倩、小飛及小傑，住在都會山的一個郊區家庭 15 年。鮑勃厭倦他的白領生活希望再重拾榮耀。有些晚上，他會和他的老朋友酷冰俠，瞞著老婆偷偷在街上行俠仗義。

（參考網站：*http://disney.wikia.com/wiki/The_Incredibles*）

Part 1

Part 2

Part 3

Part 4

 情境對話 Track 11

Jill is a business woman with 2 little children. She is going on a business trip tonight. Her neighbor introduced her a nanny called, Baros, a high school girl. It is pretty urgent. She needs to take a quick interview and tells her about the task.

Jill: So, tell me about you.

Baros: I am s tender, careful, considerate, nice, and lovely girl.

Jill: Girl, I don't want to know about your mild-mannered alter ego. I need to know if you can handle the house chores.

Baros: Yes, of course. I could clean the house, wash dishes, hang out clothing...

Jill: I will be away for 7 days. You need to take care of my 2 children. One is 3 and the other is 5.

Baros: I can totally handle anything those two kids can dish out.

Jill: OK, I bought some food in the fridge. There are a lot of leftovers that you can reheat.

Baros: I am a good cook myself.

Jill: Here is my phone number. Give me a call if you have any problems.

Baros: Bon voyage.

▶▶ 中譯

吉兒是個有兩個孩子的職業婦女。她今晚要去出差。她的鄰居介紹她一個高中女孩，巴蘿絲。事情急迫，她要趕快面試並告訴她工作內容。

吉　兒：告訴我有關於你的部分。

巴蘿絲：我是個很溫柔、小心、體貼、好相處、可愛的女孩。

吉　兒：女孩，我不想知道妳溫良恭謹的內在。我需要知道妳可以處理家事嗎？

巴蘿絲：當然。我可以清理房子、洗盤子、晾衣服……

吉　兒：我會出門 7 天。你需要照顧我一個 3 歲、一個 5 歲的孩子。

巴蘿絲：我可以完全處理任何那兩個孩子能搞出的事。

吉　兒：好，我買了一些食物在冰箱。那有很多剩菜可以加熱。

巴蘿絲：我也是個好廚師。

吉　兒：這是我的電話號碼，如果有問題，聯絡我。

巴蘿絲：旅途愉快。

單字片語解析

🚩 **mild-mannered** *adj.* 溫良恭謹的

The super star's mild-mannered temper favored her fans.

那個超級明星溫良恭謹的脾氣受她的粉絲喜愛。

🚩 **alter ego** *ph.* 內在

Check alter ego and ask yourself what you exactly want.

省察內在，問你自己到底想要甚麼。

🚩 **leftover** *n.* 剩菜

There were plenty leftovers from the party last night.

昨晚派對有很多剩菜。

你還可以這樣說

★ dish out 發生；給予

也可以這樣說 give out

The Saint can give out what others cannot. （那聖人給予很多其他人無法給的。）

★ deliver

Mailmen deliver letters to individuals. （郵差將信件個別遞送。）

★ happen

Mothers will not allow anything happens to their children.
（媽媽們不會允許任何事發生在她孩子身上。）

★ mete out

The bartender metes out the glass of cocktail.（那個酒保給了那杯雞尾酒。）

★ come about

The company comes about bonuses to its employees.（那公司給所有雇員分紅。）

生活知識小補給

這世界真有超人嗎？看超人故事，總是勾起我們無限想像，我好想像鮑勃一樣的無窮力氣，像海倫的超級彈性，像小倩一樣可以隱形，像小飛一樣健步如飛和像小傑一樣的可以變形……如果我們可以許願，我倒是很希望有一雙可以飛翔的翅膀。我可以隨時飛到我朋友身邊，給予幫助，我不開心時，可以飛翔天上，飛到開心的國度。也許我想多了，呵呵，你想要甚麼超能力呢？

Unit 12

超人特攻隊
I'm With You For Better Or Worse.

動畫經典佳句

"What a trooper, I'm proud of you."
你好強，我以你為榮。

"They won't exercise restraint because you are children."
他們不會因為你是孩子而對你手下留情。

"Super-duper, Dad! I'm with you for better or worse."
超出色的，爸！我和你禍福與共。

動畫內容敘述

Bob and Helen have superpowers, their children, Violet and Dash also have innate superpowers. Violet is able to create force fields and turn invisible, and Dash is able to run at exceptionally high speeds, but the toddler Jack-Jack has yet to show any. One day, Bob loses his temper when his supervisor refuses to let him stop a mugging, revealing his super strength and causing him to lose his job. While trying to figure out what to tell Helen, Bob finds a message from a mysterious woman named Mirage, who asks for Mr. Incredible's help to stop a savage tripod-like robot called the Omnidroid on a distant island for an incredible reward.

　　鮑勃和海倫有超能力，他們的孩子小倩和小飛天生也有超能力。小倩能製造能量場，並隱形。小飛能跑得超快，而小傑的能力仍未看出來。一天，鮑勃很生氣他的老闆不讓他去阻止搶劫，因而顯露了他的超能力，讓他被炒魷魚。正在擔心該如何告訴海倫，鮑勃發現一個叫幻影的女人給他的訊息，她要求鮑勃幫她阻止在遙遠島嶼的一個三腳超能機器人，並承諾給他一個極優渥的報酬。

（參考網站：http://disney.wikia.com/wiki/The_Incredibles）

1
Part

2
Part

3
Part

4
Part

情境對話 Track 12

Tony, father and son, Monroe, join a World Robot Competition. They hope they can win the gold medal this time. Though, they failed in the past few years. They have exercised for a long time. It comes to the final.

Tony: We have to be very careful in the final. They won't exercise restraint because you are children.

Monroe: Sure, Dad. I will try with all my strength.

Tony: Meanwhile, you should rehearse what to say during oral.

Monroe: I have practiced a thousand times at home. I am sure I comprehend all the details of our robot.

Tony: Then, just stay calm and be ready.

Monroe: Super-duper, Dad! I'm with you for better or worse.
(At the closing ceremony)

Tony: What a trooper. I'm proud of you.

Monroe: It only works only if all the little cogs mesh together.

Tony: They finally recognize our talents.

Monroe: It's the artificial intelligence that enables it to solve any problem.

Tony: I'm calling to celebrate a momentous occasion.

▸▸ **中譯**

爸爸東尼和兒子門羅參加世界機器人大賽。他們希望這次可以得冠軍，雖然他們在前幾年都失敗了。他們已經練習了很久，終於到決賽了。

東尼：在決賽時，我們一定要很小心。他們不會因為你是孩子而對你手下留情。

門羅：好的，爸。我會盡全力。

東尼：現在，你應該排練口試時要說什麼。

門羅：我已經在家練過一千次了，我確定我完全了解我們機器人的一切細節。

東尼：那就保持平靜準備就緒。

門羅：超讚的，爸！我和你禍福與共。

（在閉幕式）

東尼：你好強，我以你為榮。

門羅：只有所有小齒輪一起運作才會成功。

東尼：他們最後終於認可我們的天分。

門羅：是人工智慧讓機器人能解決所有問題。

東尼：讓我們慶祝這個重要的時刻吧！

1 Part

2 Part

3 Part

4 Part

單字片語解析

🚩 **trooper** 　*n.*　騎兵

The troopers marched across the border.

這個軍隊行軍通過邊界。

🚩 **proud of** 　*ph.*　以…為榮

I am so proud of being part of this team.

我很榮幸成為這個團隊的一員。

🚩 **exercise** 　*n.*　練習；操練

The military practice exercises near the mountain.

軍隊在山邊做軍事演習。

你還可以這樣說

★ for better or worse 禍福與共

也可以這樣說 share thick and thin with

Fanny promises to share thick and thin with Richard.（芬妮承諾要與李察禍福與共。）

★ go through thick and thin together

Madam Teresa went through thick and thin together with her followers.（德雷莎修女與她的跟隨者禍福與共。）

★ super-duper 出色的

也可以這樣說 outstanding

Teachers were impressed with their outstanding perfor-mance.（老師對她們的優異表現印象深刻。）

★ excellent

The robot designed by those young scientists is excellent.

（由這一群年輕科學家設計的機器人真是太棒了。）

★ What a trooper! 你好強

也可以這樣說 You are marvelous!（你真的不可思議！）

生活知識小補給

　　世界最快的飛毛腿，要數世界紀錄保持人「牙買加閃電」柏特，他在北京奧運，再度證明他自己是「世界上跑得最快的人」。他的跑步速度為 100 公尺（9.58 秒）與 200 公尺（19.19 秒）。我想這應該是人類目前的極速。而世界上跑得最快的動物，是居住在非洲撒哈拉沙漠南部的獵豹(cheetah)。獵豹極速最高可達每小時 112 公里。換算起來，19.19 秒可以跑 595 公尺，遠遠快過人類 3 倍呀。

2
Part

友情愛情

Unit 1

冰雪奇緣
I Am Not Buying It.

👑 動畫經典佳句

"I got engaged, but then she freaked out, because I'd only just met him, you know, that day."
我訂婚了,然後她傻住了,因為我才剛認識他,你知道,當天。

"She said she wouldn't bless the marriage."
她說她不會祝福這段婚姻。

"You have friends who are love experts. I am not buying it."
你有朋友是愛情專家。我才不信。

動畫內容敘述

When Elsa comes of age, the kingdom prepares for her coronation. Excited to be allowed out of the castle again, Princess Anna explores the town and meets Prince Hans of the Southern Isles; the two quickly develop a mutual attraction. During the reception, Hans proposes to Anna, who hastily accepts. However, Elsa refuses to grant her blessing and forbids their sudden marriage. The sisters argue, culminating in the exposure of Elsa's abilities in an emotional outburst. Elsa flees the castle, vowing to never return. Meanwhile, Anna sets out in search of her sister, determines to return her to Arendelle. While obtaining supplies, Anna meets an iceman named Kristoff and his reindeer, Sven, and convinces Kristoff to guide her up the North Mountain.

當艾莎到達一定的年紀，王國為她準備登基大典。安娜公主因為可以離開城堡出去玩覺得很興奮，她探索城市，遇見來自南島的漢斯王子，兩人很快地彼此互相吸引。在歡迎會時，漢斯對安娜求婚，安娜草率地答應了。然而，艾莎拒絕給予祝福並阻止他們如此突然的婚姻。這對姊妹因此吵架，使得艾莎因情緒的爆發而暴露了她的特異能力。艾莎逃到城堡，發誓不再回去。同時，安娜出發去尋找她的姐姐，決定把她帶回來。在準備補給時，安娜碰到一位採冰人斯基托夫及他的馴鹿小斯，並說服斯基托夫帶她到北山去。

（參考網站：*http://disney.wikia.com/wiki/Frozen*）

 情境對話 👧 Track 13

Dora has been looking for love for many years. She is desperate for love. One day, she met a handsome man, Fred, at the park near her house. They had a happy short talk. Dora has a crush on him and she believes he is her Mr. Right. She shared the good news with her mother and told her excitedly that she is gonna marry the man. Nevertheless, her mother was not very happy about her decision. Dora is upset and calls her best friend Cathy.

Dora: I need your advice.

Cathy: What's up?

Dora: I met a man in the park. I told my mum the good news about us, but she was mad at me.

Cathy: What? Gosh! What happened?

Dora: I got engaged, but then she freaked out, because I'd only just met him, you know, that day.

Cathy: You were engaged on the day, weren't you?

Dora: Mum said she wouldn't bless the marriage. Well, I am very upset. Tell me what I should do.

Cathy: I have a friend who is a love expert. I wonder if you'd like to meet him.

Dora: You have a friend who is a love expert. I am not buying it.

Cathy: No kidding. Let me take you to him. He will give you good advice.

▶▶ **中譯**

朵拉尋找愛情許多年。她超渴望愛情。一天，她在家附近的公園遇見一位很帥的男人佛列德，他們有一段很愉快的短暫聊天。朵拉煞到他了，她相信他就是她的真命天子。她把這消息和她的媽媽分享，並告訴媽媽，她將要嫁給這個男人。然而，媽媽對她的決定並不高興。朵拉很沮喪並打電話給她的好友凱西。

朵拉：我需要建議。

凱西：怎麼了？

朵拉：我在公園遇見一個男人。我跟我媽說這個好消息，但是她好生氣。

凱西：甚麼？天呀！發生甚麼事？

朵拉：我訂婚了，然後她傻住了，因為我才剛認識他，你知道，當天。

凱西：你當天就訂婚了，不是吧？

朵拉：我媽說她不會祝福這段婚姻。嗯，我很難過。告訴我，我要怎麼辦。

凱西：我有個朋友是愛情專家。我不知道你是否有興趣要跟他見見面。

朵拉：你有朋友是愛情專家。我才不信。

凱西：沒跟你開玩笑。我帶你去見他。他會給你建議的。

1
Part

2
Part

3
Part

4
Part

087

單字片語解析

engage *v.* 使訂婚
Jay is engaged to Janice.
杰和珍妮絲訂婚了。

bless *v.* 為…祝福
The couple was blessed.
那對夫婦被祝福。

marriage *n.* 婚姻
The old lady has a wonderful marriage.
那位老太太有一個很讚的婚姻。

expert *n.* 專家
We need an expert to help out.
我們需要一名專家來幫我們擺脫困境。

buy *v.* 接受
If he proposes to me, I will buy it.
如果他向我求婚,我會接受。

freak out *ph.* 嚇壞了
I freak out on hearing the news.
我聽到那新聞嚇壞了。

你還可以這樣說

★ freak out 嚇呆了

也可以這麼說 lose one's nerve

I lost my nerve when I heard the news.（當我聽到這消息我整個人嚇呆了。）

★ gross out

His behavior grossed me out.（他的舉動嚇壞了我。）

★ I am not buying it. 我不信

也可以這麼說 I'm not going to believe it.

He said he could reverse the situation. I'm not going to believe it.（他說他可以翻轉情勢。我才不信。）

生活知識小補給

　　現在網路非常方便，異國戀情也隨之昌盛。這樣僅有一面之緣，甚至未見面即約定結婚的情侶也越來越多。常常我們把這樣的戀情稱為 cyber love。這樣的戀情，究竟穩不穩固，足以成為家庭而共度下半生？根據專家統計，離婚的機率非常的高。決定進入婚姻是神聖的，兩個因愛情結合的男女，其實對彼此及家庭有相當的認識是必要的，因為將來生養子女，就是一輩子的責任與承諾呢！

Unit 2

怪獸大學
I Am Your Roomie.

"I am your roomie. I can tell we're going to be the best chums."

我是你的室友,我可以感覺到,我們將會成為最好的朋友。

"Take whatever bed you want; I want you to have first dibs."

選你要的床,我要你優先。

"What you did today was insane. That was awesome!"

你今天做的好瘋狂,超讚的!

動畫內容敘述

Mike arrives at Monsters University and is extremely excited. After taking a picture card for his ID and visiting his school, he finally goes to his room, meets and befriends his roommate, the nerdy and shy Randall Randy Boggs, who has trouble controlling his invisibility power. When Randy suddenly disappears while greeting his new friend, Mike is impressed and tells Randy to use it more, to the Chameleon's shock. Randy soon gets rid of his glasses under Mike's suggestion because they don't turn invisible when he does. While Randy is worried about not being able to impress the cool kids, Mike is laid back and confident in his scaring abilities.

　　麥可進入怪獸大學非常興奮。在拿到學生證及參觀學校後，他到了宿舍，和他的室友見面及交朋友。那像書呆子又害羞的藍道，不大會控制他的隱形能力。當藍道向他的新朋友打招呼時突然消失了，麥可印象深刻，並告訴藍道要多運用這種變色龍的震撼。藍道也在麥可的建議下把眼鏡拿掉，因為它們不會在他隱形時也跟著隱形。然而當藍道擔心他不能讓孩子們印象深刻時，麥可則是對他的嚇人功夫很有自信。

（參考網站：http://disney.wikia.com/wiki/Monsters_University）

1 Part

2 Part

3 Part

4 Part

 情境對話　Track 14

Derik is a freshman. On his first day to the University, he introduced himself to his new classmates with magic tricks. Everyone was impressed. After the whole day activities, he went back to his dorm. There is a boy called Eric.

Eric:　I am your roomie. I can tell we're going to be the best chums.

Derik: Hey, I am Derik.

Eric:　I remember you. We are classmates.

Derik: Which bed do you like to take?

Eric:　Take whatever bed you want; I want you to have first dibs.

Derik: Oh, it's so nice of you.

Eric:　What you did today was insane.

Derik: Do you like it?

Eric:　That was awesome!

Derik: Would you like to learn? That's called a coin trick.

Eric:　I would love to make as much as money out of that trick.

Derik: No, that's only a trick. You have to prepare equal amounts of money.

Eric:　Well, whatever. You promise?

Derik: You bet!

▶▶ 中譯

戴瑞克是個大學新鮮人。第一天到學校，他以魔術向新同學介紹自己。每個人對他印象深刻。經過整天活動之後，他回到宿舍。房裡有一個叫艾瑞克的男孩。

艾瑞克：我是你的室友，我可以感覺到，我們將會成為最好的朋友。

戴瑞克：嗨，我是戴瑞克。

艾瑞克：我記得你。我們是同學。

戴瑞克：你要睡哪張床？

艾瑞克：選你要的床，我要你優先。

戴瑞克：喔，你人真好。

艾瑞克：你今天做的好瘋狂。

戴瑞克：你喜歡嗎？

艾瑞克：超讚的！

戴瑞克：你想要學嗎？那叫銅板魔術。

艾瑞克：我要變出好多好多錢。

戴瑞克：不，那只是魔術。你要準備同樣數量的錢。

艾瑞克：好吧，隨便。你答應的喔！

戴瑞克：那當然！

單字片語解析

roomie *n.* 室友

We are roomie now, so we have to share the rent.

我們現在是室友了，所以我們必須分擔房租。

chum *n.* 好友

Janice is my childhood chum.

珍妮絲是我小時候的玩伴。

whatever *pron.* 任何事物

I will win whatever it takes.

不論需要甚麼代價，我將贏得勝利。

dibs *n.* 權利

I have the dibs for the last run.

我在遊戲的最後一輪有權利。

insane *adj.* 瘋狂的

It is totally insane to sail during typhoon.

在颱風期間去航行真是瘋狂。

awesome *adj.* 令人敬畏的；很棒

The show was awesome.

那個表演超讚的。

你還可以這樣說

★ roomie 室友

也可以這樣說 roommate

My roommate is very noisy.（我的室友好吵。）

★ insane 瘋狂，愚蠢

也可以這樣說 crazy

He is crazy about jigsaw puzzles.（他對拼圖非常狂熱。）

★ foolish

How foolish I was to do so!（我這麼做真是愚蠢呀！）

★ mad

It is mad to climb Himalaya in such bad weather.（這樣的壞天氣去爬喜馬拉雅山真是瘋了。）

生活知識小補給

　　住宿是件令人期待又怕受傷害的事。大一新鮮人最開心，以為住宿後從此脫離父母，可以和朋友歡樂過生活，卻發現事實並非如此。筆者當年有一位可愛的室友，她很難被喚醒，於是準備了一個超大的鬧鐘，這一台鬧鐘的起床號可以比擬選舉用的大聲公。她怕起不來，常常設定上課一個半小時前喚醒。結果，不幸的是把所有室友嚇醒，而她仍安然好夢。唉，其實家還是永遠是最溫暖的地方呢！

動畫經典佳句

"Hey there, teammates! Come on aboard!"

嘿，夥伴，歡迎加入！

"Guys, one slip-up on the next event, and we are goners."

老兄，下一次失手，我們就完了。

"You'll never know what it's like to fail because you were born a Sullivan!"

你不知甚麼是失敗，因為你是天生的蘇利文！

動畫內容敘述

They are nearly found by the policemen. Without losing time, the two of them hurry back into the bungalow and open the wardrobe, but find out that the door must have been shut down. Hardscrabble orders the entire room cleared out until the authorities arrive. In the bungalow, the policemen are getting closer. Mike thinks that, if they can generate enough scream energy, they can activate the door from their side. It's their only chance, but Sulley has his doubt. He may be good at scaring children, but these policemen are adults and adults usually cannot be scared. Mike knows every scare tactic in the book, so they have a chance.

　　他們差一點被警察找到。沒有浪費時間，他們兩個快速回到小屋，並打開衣櫥，但發現那扇門已經被關閉。郝刻薄院長命令清空整個房間，直到當局到來。在小屋內，警察越來越靠近。麥可想，若他們可以蒐集足夠的尖叫能量，他們可以從他們這一邊啟動門。這是他們唯一的機會，但蘇利文懷疑。他可能很會嚇小孩，但這群警察是大人，大人通常不會被嚇到。麥可知道書中的每一個嚇人技巧，所以他們還有機會。

（參考網站：http://disney.wikia.com/wiki/Monsters_University）

 情境對話 Track 15

Leon is on the rugby team in school. One of their teammates got injured during the tournament. Rick was introduced by their coach and said he is from the rugby family. Rick is not very confident on himself because he thinks himself as a nerd. They don't have time to consider if he is in or not.

Leon: Hey there, teammate! Come on aboard!

Rick: Hi, I only played rugby when I was in elementary school.

Leon: Now, we get even with the other team.

Rick: What can I help with now?

Leon: One slip-up on the next event, and we are goners.

Rick: Gee, I only know the game, but I am not as good as my dad.

Leon: He is a hero to us.

Rick: I know he is very game, but not me...

Leon: Come on. You'll never know what it's like to fail because you were born a rugby player!

Rick: I will try my best, but I just cannot promise.
(After the tournament)

Leon: That was cool, Rick, your last kick saved us. That was awesome!

Rick: Thank you, mate.

▸▸ 中譯

里歐是學校橄欖球隊員。他們其中一個隊員在比賽中受傷了。瑞克被教練介紹進來並說他來自橄欖球世家。瑞克對自己很沒有信心，因為他認為自己是個書呆子。他們沒有時間考慮他是否加入或不加入。

里歐：嘿，夥伴，歡迎加入！

瑞克：嘿，我只有在小學時玩過橄欖球。

里歐：現在，我們和另一隊打成平手。

瑞克：我現在可以幫甚麼忙？

里歐：下一次失手，我們就完了。

瑞克：天呀，我只知道如何打，但我沒有像我爸爸打得那麼好。

里歐：他是我們心中的英雄耶。

瑞克：我知道他很棒，但是不是我⋯⋯

里歐：別這樣，你不知甚麼是失敗，因為你是天生的橄欖球員！

瑞克：我會認真打，但是我不能承諾甚麼。

　　　（比賽完後）

里歐：超讚的，瑞克，你的臨門一腳救了我們。太棒了！

瑞克：謝謝你，夥伴。

單字片語解析

▶ **teammate** *n.* 隊友
Be nice to your teammate.
對你的隊友好一點。

▶ **aboard** *adv.* 上（船、飛機、車）
It's time to go aboard.
上飛機的時間到。

▶ **slip-up** *n.* 出差錯
It must be a slip-up somewhere.
這一定是哪裡出差錯了。

▶ **goner** *n.* 無可挽救的（人）事
You will be a goner if you fail the test.
如果你考試沒過，你就沒救了。

▶ **fail** *v.* 失敗；不及格
He failed the attempt.
他在嘗試中失敗了。

▶ **born** *adj.* 天生的
Marilyn Monroe was a born super star.
瑪麗蓮夢露是個天生的超級明星。

你還可以這樣說

★ slip-up 出差錯

也可以這樣說 boo-boo

He made a boo-boo in his report.（他在報告中出了一個愚蠢的大錯。）

★ error

There is an error in this calculation.（這個計算有一個錯誤。）

★ born 天生的

也可以這樣說 gifted

The boy is gifted in painting.（那男孩很有繪畫的天份。）

★ talented

Jack is a talented engineer.（杰克是個有天賦的工程師。）

生活知識小補給

　　何為團隊精神？我們為什麼需要團隊呢？就像是行駛一輛腳踏車，每一組零件都不一樣，也有不同功能，若少了一個零件，即使有再美麗的外表，也是破銅爛鐵，無法發揮作用。每一個人都有不同的特性，在團隊中，每個人必須貢獻自己所長，學習無私的付出，才能讓團隊達到很好的目標。這世界上有許多很強的國家，民族的團隊精神就很令人讚賞，像是美國、日本。珍惜你的隊友也是一門非常重要的學習喔！

1 Part

2 Part

3 Part

4 Part

食破天驚
The Fate of World Is Depending On Us.

👑 動畫經典佳句

"The fate of world is depending on us."
世界的命運取決於我們。

"A bully turned friend will be a friend to the end."
惡霸變成朋友將是一輩子朋友。（中文諺語）

"Sometimes I wish I kept my bullies around. So I could crush them with my success."
有時候我希望我能把羞辱留在身邊，這樣我就我能以我的成就粉碎它們。

情境簡介

Citizens and worldly tourists in Chewandswallow are blissful until suddenly a large tornado formed of spaghetti and meatballs threatens the town. Flint rushes to his lab to turn the FLDSMDFR off and attempts to send a "kill code" to stop the machine, but the mayor destroys the communication device by throwing a giant radish at it before he can do it. With Flint unable to control the machine, a massive food storm is created which threatens the world. When Flint's father encourages him to fix the mess, Flint gains self-confidence, places the kill code in a USB flash drive, and build s a new flying car to reach and deactivate the FLDSMDFR, with the aid of Sam, her cameraman Manny, Steve and Brent.

市民及世界的遊客在美食小島很快樂，直到突然間一陣由義大利麵及貢丸所形成的龍捲風威脅這個城鎮為止。富林跑到實驗室關掉富拉美食複機，並企圖傳送「死亡密碼」來停止機器，但是市長在他採取行動之前丟了一個巨大的白蘿蔔破壞通訊設備。富林無法控制機器，巨大的食物風暴威脅這個世界。富林的父親鼓勵他處理這一團混亂，富林獲得了自信，將死亡密碼放在隨身硬碟快速驅動器內，並建造一台飛行汽車，在珊、她的攝影師曼尼、史帝夫及布萊特的幫助下，到達並阻止了富拉美食複機。

（參考網站：https://en.wikipedia.org/wiki/Cloudy_with_a_Chance_of_Meatballs_(film)）

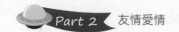 

情境對話　Track 16

Benny is often bullied by his classmates. He is extremely upset. His mother tries to comfort him and talks to him after dinner.

Mother: How is your school?

Benny: I hate school. I don't understand why they always try to find fault with me.

Mother: Have you ever said "no" to them?

Benny: No, I was so scared.

Mother: You are too nice and too timid to express your feelings.

Benny: But they are stronger, I do not know how to fight.

Mother: What are you gonna do? You should do something to solve the problem.

Benny: I want to be very successful and to be on top of the class.

Mother: Why?

Benny: I don't want them to look down on me. Sometimes I wish I kept my bullies around, so I could crush them with my success.

Mother: That's a very good motivation, but do not bear hatred all the time.

Benny: I believe that's the only solution.

Mother: A Chinese saying goes, "A bully turned friend will be a friend to the end."

Benny: Do you really believe so?

Mother: Yes, I grew up this way. It works. Fate depends on us.

Benny: Thanks mum. I will try my best.

▶▶ 中譯

班尼常常被同學霸凌,他非常的沮喪。他的母親在晚餐後試著安慰他,並和他談天。

媽媽:學校還好嗎?

班尼:我討厭學校。我不懂他們為什麼一直找我碴。

媽媽:你曾試過對他們說「不」嗎?

班尼:沒有,我很害怕。

媽媽:你太好也太膽小,不敢表達你的感受。

班尼:可是他們都比較壯,我不知道如何吵架。

媽媽:你要怎麼做呢?你應該做一些事來解決問題呀。

班尼:我要很成功,也要成為班上的翹楚。

媽媽:為什麼?

班尼:我不要他們看不起我。有時候我希望我能把羞辱留在身邊,這樣我就能以我的成就粉碎它們。

媽媽:這是很好的動力,但是不要一直把仇恨掛在心上。

班尼:我相信這是唯一的答案。

媽媽:有一句中國諺語說:「惡霸變成朋友將是一輩子朋友。」

班尼:妳真的這麼認為?

媽媽:是的,我是這樣長大的。真的有用。命運取決於我們自己。

班尼:謝謝,媽,我盡我所能。

單字片語解析

🏴 **fate** *n.* 命運

She deserves a better fate.

她應該過比較好的命。

🏴 **depend** *v.* 依賴

If the activity will continue depends on the weather.

活動是否將要繼續取決於天氣。

🏴 **bully** *n.* 惡霸

Do not be afraid of the bully.

不要害怕那個惡霸。

🏴 **turn** *v.* 翻轉

Turn right when you see the traffic light.

當你看到紅綠燈右轉。

🏴 **crush** *v.* 壓碎

You can crush the walnut with a nutcracker.

你可以用核桃夾壓碎核桃。

🏴 **success** *n.* 成功

Their team reached a great success.

他們的團隊獲得極大的成功。

你還可以這樣說

★ depend on 依賴

也可以這麼說 rely on

We cannot not just rely on our luck and do nothing.（我們不能只是依賴運氣，而不做任何事。）

★ lean on

He is trustworthy; we can lean on his suggestions.（他值得信賴，我們可以依賴他的建議。）

★ be dependent on

The harvest is dependent on the weather.（收成要依賴天氣。）

生活知識小補給

　　面對學校霸凌事件的興起，我們是否真心去關懷霸凌事件的原由。被霸凌者的個性，及施暴者的心態。筆者曾經處理過校園霸凌事件，發現受霸凌孩子普遍不會勇敢表達自己的不悅，讓霸凌者以得勝的心態，持續施暴。我常常教導被霸凌者如何學習保護自己，解決問題，改變自己，往往收到比去制止施暴者行為收到更大的功效。若您是被霸凌者，想想如何解決問題，才能讓自己處於上風。

1
Part

2
Part

3
Part

4
Part

Unit 5

食破天驚2
Stew Offered By A Bully Is Poisoned Broth.

動畫經典佳句

"Stew offered by a bully is poisoned broth."
惡棍給的東西一定有毒。（中文諺語）

"You're heading into the deepest, darkest part of the jungle."
你正走進叢林最深最黑暗的地方。

"A bully can never be your friend."
惡棍永遠不能成為朋友。（中文諺語）

動畫內容敘述

Chester told Flint as they swing through the lab, collecting equipment. "Hanging from my underpants in this space brings back so many memories. Unfortunately they were not happy ones. I, too, built my lab up high to keep the bullies out" Chester said. Flint is a kind-hearted, wacky, funny, hyperactive, friendly, humorous, random, fun-loving, energetic, intelligent and creative inventor. As a child, he was a prodigy and had dreams of becoming an inventor. Unfortunately, being bullied his entire life and having strained relationship with his father has made him very attention-seeking, nervous, and is willing to go to dangerous risks just to impress or make friends with people.

當他們盪過實驗室，蒐集設備時，阿奇師告訴富林：「在這個空間，用我的內褲吊著，帶給我許多回憶。很不幸的，都不是愉快的回憶。我，也是，把實驗室弄得這麼高，是為了把惡霸趕走。」阿奇師說。富林是一個心腸好、古怪的、有趣的、過動的、友善的、幽默的、隨性的、愛玩的、充滿能量的、聰明的、及有創造力的發明家。當他還是小孩時，他就是個天才，並夢想成為一個發明家。很不幸地，他的一生都被霸凌，而且跟父親的關係緊張，這讓他變得非常愛尋求注意、焦慮，很想要以冒險來使人印象深刻或交朋友。

（參考網站：https://en.wikipedia.org/wiki/Cloudy_with_a_Chance_of_Meatballs_2）

1 Part

2 Part

3 Part

4 Part

 情境對話 Track 17

Andy is a freshman. He met some bullies in the school. He did not know they are bullies until he saw them bullying a friend of his, Gary, on the playground. Gary was his good friend while they were in high school. One day, he met Gary on the street. Gary warned him.

Gary: Andy, I heard that you are one of the bullies.

Andy: No, definitely not. I did not know they are bullies.

Gary: You had better stay away from them. You're heading into the deepest, darkest part of the jungle.

Andy: They are not as bad as you think.

Gary: You don't understand. A bully can never be your friend.

Andy: I have hung out with them. They treated me like a buddy. They gave me a lot of gifts.

Gary: Stew offered by a bully is poisoned broth. If you don't think you are one of them.

Andy: What did they do to you that day?

Gary: They threatened me to offer some money to them.

Andy: Really? I will be very careful. Thank you for your advice.

▶▶ 中譯

安迪是個新鮮人。他在學校認識一些惡棍。他不知道他們是惡棍,直到有一天看到他們在操場霸凌他的朋友蓋瑞。蓋瑞是他中學時的好朋友。一天,他在路上遇見蓋瑞。蓋瑞警告他。

蓋瑞:安迪,我聽説你是其中的一個惡棍。

安迪:不,絕對不是。我不知道他們是惡棍。

蓋瑞:你最好離他們遠一點。你正走進叢林最深最黑暗的地方。

安迪:他們沒你想像得那麼壞。

蓋瑞:你不懂,惡棍永遠不能成為朋友。

安迪:我跟他們出去過。他們對我就像兄弟一樣。他們給我很多禮物呢!

蓋瑞:惡棍給的東西一定有毒。如果你不認為你是他們的一員。

安迪:那一天他們對你做甚麼?

蓋瑞:他們威脅我提供一些錢給他們。

安迪:真的嗎?我要很小心。謝謝你的建議。

單字片語解析

stew *n.* 燉肉

The stew made by the chef tastes wonderful.

那個廚師做的燉肉嚐起來很好吃。

offer *v.* 提供

The company offers me a job opportunity.

那家公司提供我一個工作的機會。

poison *n.* 毒藥

Pesticide is a poison.

殺蟲劑是個毒藥。

你還可以這樣說

★ offer 提供

也可以這麼說 provide

Lunch will be provided in the meeting. （在會議中會提供午餐。）

★ present

The secretary needs to present all the necessary documents. （那秘書需要提供所有需要的文件。）

★ head 出發；去

也可以這麼說 move toward

Let's move toward the mountain.（讓我們出發到山上去。）

★ proceed

He proceeds to the next agenda.（他進行到下一個議程。）

★ go

The bushman goes into the jungle.（那個住在叢林的人走進叢林裡了。）

生活知識小補給

　　交朋友是件讓人愉快的事，但是朋友的好壞，如何選擇，是人一輩子的課題。若是同班同學，你沒有選擇，但是從學習的態度及交作業的認真程度，你可以窺知同學的特性。除卻教室外呢？一般人多會選擇加入社團，因為在同一個社團內，會尋找到共同興趣的朋友，比如棋藝、登山、戲劇、電影…等等正當休閒娛樂，也比較不會有像上面故事中的安迪，誤交損友的危機了。

1 Part

2 Part

3 Part

4 Part

腦筋急轉彎

He Is Making That Stupid Face Again.

動畫經典佳句

"This isn't a date, is it?"

這不是個約會，不是嗎？

"Mum, it's not a date. We are going skating with a group of friends."

媽，這不是約會啦！我們要跟一群朋友一起去溜冰。

"He is making that stupid face again."

"Come on, he is adorable."

他又再扮那個愚蠢的臉。

別這麼說嘛！他很討人喜歡。

動畫內容敘述

Jordan is a boy who Riley meets at a hockey rink. One day, Jordan shows up to take Riley out skating, her parents suspect their daughter is going out on a date. While Jill goes upstairs to ask Riley, Bill stays downstairs with Jordan. Both the parents' emotions don't agree with what's afoot, especially Bill's. He gives Jordan the silent treatment but he doesn't react. He next tries intimidation, but only gets a slight chuckle from Jordan. However, the two end up bonding over their experiences in a band and love for music. Later, Riley and Jordan leave for the skate, leaving Jill and Bill satisfied that Jordan is a good kid.

喬登是萊莉在曲棍球場遇見的男孩。一天喬登來約萊莉一起去溜冰，她的父母懷疑女兒要出去約會。媽媽吉兒上樓找萊莉時，爸爸比爾在樓下陪喬登。父母都感到不是很愉快，特別是比爾。他安靜地對待喬登，但他沒反應。他接著威嚇他，卻得到一個輕輕的發笑聲。最後兩個人因在樂團的經驗及喜歡音樂的興趣而聊得很愉快。最後，萊莉和喬登去溜冰，比爾和吉兒滿意喬登是個好孩子。

（參考網站：http://disney.wikia.com/wiki/Inside_Out）

1 Part

2 Part

3 Part

4 Part

 情境對話 Track 18

Mike is very popular in the school. Almost every girl in the school dreams to go out with him. Sarah is organizing a skating tournament. Mike signs in for the game. For a while, they go skating with friends and practice for the tournament. Today, Mike knocks on the door of Sarah's, which makes Sarah's mother nervous.

Mum: Hi, dear, Mike is at the door.

Sarah: Tell him, I will be there soon.

Mum: Where are you guys going?

Sarah: We are going to go skating with a group of friends.

Mum: This isn't a date, is it?

Sarah: Mum, it's not a date. You know the tournament will be held in a week. We are all so excited about it. Joe, Sandy, Harry, Una and Janice will go skating rink together.

Mum: Oh, you do dream to go out with him, don't you?

Sarah: Mum... Come on! It's not like that.

Mum: Well, he is adorable. If I were you, I would...

Sarah: Mum, keep daydreaming, I will see you tonight.

▸▸ 中譯

麥可在學校非常受歡迎,學校裡的每個女孩都夢想跟他約會。莎拉正在策劃一場溜冰比賽,麥可也報名參加。他們和朋友為了比賽練習溜冰一陣子,今天麥可來找莎拉,讓莎拉的媽媽非常緊張。

媽　：嗨,親愛的,麥可在門口了。

莎拉：告訴他,我馬上來。

媽　：你們要去哪裡?

莎拉：我們要跟一群朋友去溜冰。

媽　：這不是約會吧,不是嗎?

莎拉：媽,這不是約會,你知道再一個星期就要比賽了,我們都很期待。喬伊、珊狄、哈瑞、鄔娜和珍妮絲都會一起去溜冰場。

媽　：喔,妳一直夢想跟他一起出去,不是嗎?

莎拉：媽……拜託!不是那樣的。

媽　：嗯,他很討人喜歡。如果我是你,我一定……

莎拉：媽,繼續做你的白日夢,晚上見。

單字片語解析

date *n.* 日子、約會、棗子

Kelly went on a blind date under the request of her parents.

凱莉在父母的要求下去相親。

adorable *adj.* 值得崇拜的

Bill is adorable for his devotion to medical science.

比爾在醫學上的貢獻值得尊敬。

hockey rink *n.* 曲棍球場

Those kids are playing at a hockey rink.

那些孩子正在曲棍球場玩。

make face *ph.* 扮鬼臉

The boy made his face to his nanny.

那個男孩對著他的保母扮鬼臉。

come on *ph.* 快吧！少來！

Come on, shake a leg. We should hurry up now.

快吧！趕快走，我們要加快速度了。

go skating 溜冰

I would rather go skating than hiking.

我寧願去溜冰也不要去健行。

你還可以這樣說

★ make face 扮鬼臉

也可以這麼說 mug

The child mugged at the teacher.（那孩子對著老師扮鬼臉。）

★ grimace

That was a biggest grimace I have ever seen.（那是我見過最大的鬼臉。）

★ adorable 值得崇拜的；可愛的

也可以這麼說 charming

She is such a charming lady.（她是個如此迷人的女士。）

★ admirable

His achievement is admirable.（他的成就是令人欽佩的。）

生活知識小補給

　　在這一段落的電影中，我們看到父母對女兒即將與男孩外出的緊張心情，看到父親的防衛機制，生氣、警告，母親的緊張、擔心，其實都是在告訴我們，父母對子女的保護及捍衛之心，而我們常常對父母的愛和關心表現出不耐與厭煩，像萊莉的本能反應一樣。而這一連串反應，根據神經心理學的敘述，人的情緒其實都是人際關係的一連串反應呢！

119

Unit 7

羅雷司
Shame On Him.

👑 動畫經典佳句

"Behold! The intruder and his violent way, shame on him."

看哪！那個入侵者和他粗暴的方式，他真是可恥。

"Well, fortunately, you are not the target market, weirdo."

喔，幸運的是，你不是目標市場，怪物。

"You know me, just arising, putting out the vibe."

你知道我，正在興起，感覺正好。

動畫內容敘述

A boy living in a polluted town visits a strange isolated man called the Once-ler at the far end of town. The boy pays the Once-ler fifteen cents, a nail, and the shell of a great-great-great grandfather snail to explain why the area is in such a run-down state. The Once-ler explains to the boy how he once arrived in a beautiful, pristine valley containing happy, playful fauna that spent their days romping around blissfully among "Truffula trees". The Once-ler proceeded to cut down the Truffula trees to gather raw material to knit "Thneeds," a ridiculously versatile invention of his. Thneeds could be used as a shirt, a sock, a glove, a hat, a carpet, a pillow, a sheet, a curtain, a seat cover, and countless other things.

一個住在污染汙染城鎮的男孩，拜會一個住在離城鎮很遠，奇怪的孤獨老人，萬事樂。那男孩付了萬事樂 15 角，一片指甲及一個曾曾曾祖父蝸牛的殼，請他解釋為何這區域變成這樣一個耗竭的狀態。萬事樂告訴男孩他曾經到過一個漂亮、原始的村莊，裡面充滿快樂的愛玩的動物，整天在「*Truffula trees* 松露樹林」玩耍。萬事樂砍下樹做為原料，編織他不可思議的多功能發明「絲尼」。絲尼可以用來做襯衫、襪子、手套、帽子、地毯、枕頭、床單、窗簾、座椅蓋、及無數東西。

(參考網站：*https://en.wikipedia.org/wiki/The_Lorax_(film)*)

1 Part

2 Part

3 Part

4 Part

 情境對話 Track 19

A street vendor, Kevin, comes to the village. He sells a lot of beautiful candies. They are tasty and yummy. One day, Lora found out he carried a lot of strange buckets with colored water at night. She followed him secretly and discovered the color water contained poisonous pigments. She decided to reveal his attempt in front of crowd.

Lora: Behold! The intruder and his violent way, shame on him.

Kevin: On what ground do you say so?

Lora: Look at those disgusting buckets and that poisonous water.

Kevin: Well, fortunately, you are not the target market, weirdo.

Lora: Do not let him poison our children.

Kevin: You know me, just arising, putting out the vibe.

Lora: That's why I am here to warn you. If you don't leave the village, I will ask villagers against you.

Kevin: All right, don't be angry. Can we talk it over?

Lora: Unless you promise not to use color pigments.

Kevin: Ok, I will dump them right away.

▶▶ 中譯

一個街頭小販，凱文，來到村莊。他賣了一堆漂亮的糖果。它們真是好吃。一天，蘿拉發現他在晚上提了一堆裝滿各種顏色奇怪的桶子，她悄悄地跟蹤他，發現顏色水裡含有毒的顏料。她決定在群眾面前揭發他的企圖。

蘿拉：看哪！那個入侵者和他粗暴的方式，他真是可恥。

凱文：你憑甚麼這樣說？

蘿拉：看那些噁心的桶子和有毒的水。

凱文：喔，幸運的是，你不是目標市場，怪物。

蘿拉：別讓他毒害我們的孩子。

凱文：你知道我，正在興起，感覺正好。

蘿拉：這就是為什麼我要在這裡警告你。如果你不離開村莊，我會讓村民對抗你。

凱文：好好，別生氣。我們可以談和嗎？

蘿拉：除非你答應不再用色素。

凱文：好，我會馬上把它們倒掉。

單字片語解析

behold *int.* 看哪！

Behold! What a beautiful flower!

看哪！好漂亮的花呀！

intruder *n.* 侵入者

Be aware of the intruder !

小心那個入侵者！

violent *adj.* 激烈的

The violent storm struck the whole town.

暴風雨襲擊整個城鎮。

fortunately *adv.* 幸運地

He fortunately finished the project in time.

他幸運地及時完成計畫。

target *n.* 目標

I don't want to be the target of gossip.

我不想成為八卦的對象。

weirdo *n.* 怪物

He was called a weirdo by other students.

他被其他學生叫做怪物。

你還可以這樣說

★ shame on 羞辱

也可以這麼說 put...to shame 使蒙羞

His dreadful behavior put all of us to shame.（他可怕的行為讓我們蒙羞。）

★ violent 激烈的

也可以這麼說 rough

I don't like using the rough way to solve the problem.（我不喜歡用激烈的方式解決問題。）

★ fierce

Grandpa's fierce temper scares everyone.（爺爺的暴躁脾氣嚇壞每一個人。）

生活知識小補給

　　森林，正在快速的消失。當你正在閱讀這一段文字時，一個足球場的森林已經被夷為平地了。全球森林面積，每年正以減少 730 公頃的速度逐漸消失。亞馬遜雨林是地球上最大的熱帶雨林，其面積相當於美國的國土面積。世界上已知的一半物種都生活在亞馬遜流域。然而，這裡也是世界上森林消失速度最快的區域之一。巴西政府在 2006 年承認大約有 63% 來自巴西亞馬遜地區的木材是非法取得的呢！

Unit 8

北極特快車
Let's Not Dilly-Dally.

👑 **動畫經典佳句**

"There is no greater gift than friendship."
沒有任何比友誼更棒的禮物。

"Can you count on us to get you home safe and sound?"
你可以信賴我們安全且忠實地將你送回家嗎？

"No pushing. But let's not dilly-dally."
不要推，但不要閒晃。

動畫內容敘述

After the witness of Santa, the children finally return to the train. The conductor punches letters into each ticket. These letters spell some advice (such as: "Learn", "Lead", or "Believe" for the Know-it-all, Hero Girl, and Hero Boy individually). As the hero boy returns home, he sees Santa has delivered gift to Billy's house. On the Christmas morning, his sister finds a small gift hidden behind the Christmas tree. He opens the gift and discovers that is the bell he lost on the seat from Santa. When he rings, both he and his sister can hear the beautiful sound, but not his parents. Only the one who believes in the Spirit of Christmas can hear the sound.

在見證聖誕老公公後，孩子們最後回到車上。列車長在每一張車票上打文字的洞（像是：個別為萬事通、英雄女孩、英雄男孩打上「學習」、「領導」、「相信」等字）。當英雄男孩回家，他看見聖誕老公公把禮物送到比利的家。在聖誕節的早上，他的妹妹發現在聖誕樹後的一個小禮物，他打開禮物，發現裡面是聖誕老公公送給他，而卻被他遺落在椅子上的鈴鐺。當他搖鈴，他和妹妹都聽到美麗的聲音，但他的父母卻聽不見。只有相信聖誕精神的人才聽得見。

（參考網站：https://en.wikipedia.org/wiki/The_Polar_Express_(film)）

1
Part

2
Part

3
Part

4
Part

 Track 20

Garry went to the market with his mum. He is too concentrated on the games in his cell phone . Suddenly, he is aware that he has gone lost. He is too young to recognize his way home. He is merely an eight-year-old boy. Sally, a high school girl, notices him and wants to offer help. However, Garry is advised not to talk to strangers.

Sally: Are you ok? Where is your mum?

Garry: Mum told me not to talk to strangers.

Sally: Well, she may be right. But, once you need help, you do have to talk to somebody you don't know. I saw you wandering around.

Garry: I couldn't find my way home.

Sally: Where are you from?

Garry: I am from Springville.

Sally: I know Springville. It is a town about 10 miles away from here.

Garry: How can I get there?

Sally: A friend of mine has a car. Can you count on us to get you home safe and sound?

Garry: I think...I can.

Sally: A friend in need is a friend indeed. There is no greater gift than friendship.

Garry: Thank you so much.

     (Sally calls her friend for help. He arrives soon.)

Sally: Let's get into the car. No pushing. But let's not dilly-dally.

▶▶ 中譯

蓋瑞和媽媽去市場。他太專心於手機的遊戲，突然，他發現他迷路了。他太小無法認出回家的路。他只是個八歲男孩。莎莉，一個高中生，注意到他並想幫他。可是，媽媽教蓋瑞不要跟陌生人交談。

莎莉：你還好嗎？你媽媽在哪裡？

蓋瑞：媽媽告訴我不能跟陌生人講話。

莎莉：嗯，她可能是對的。但是，一旦你需要幫忙，你一定要跟你不認識的人講話。我看到你在徘徊。

蓋瑞：我找不到回家的路。

莎莉：你哪裡來的？

蓋瑞：我來自春市。

莎莉：我知道春市，它大概離這裡 10 英里遠。

蓋瑞：我要怎麼去那裡？

莎莉：我一個朋友有車。你可以信賴我們安全且忠實地將你送回家嗎？

蓋瑞：我想…我可以。

莎莉：患難見真情。沒有任何比友誼更棒的禮物。

蓋瑞：真的很謝謝你們。

    （莎莉打電話給朋友尋求協助。他很快就到了。）

莎莉：讓我們上車吧！不要推，但不要閒晃。

1 Part

2 Part

3 Part

4 Part

單字片語解析

friendship　*n.*　友誼

What he does ruins our friendship.

他所做的事破壞了我們的友誼。

count on　*ph.*　信賴

You can count on me.

你可以信賴我。

safe　*adj.*　安全的

It is not safe to stand under a tree while raining.

下雨時站在樹下不安全。

你還可以這樣說

★ count on 信賴

也可以這麼説 depend on

He is an expert. We have to depend on his judgment.（他是一個專家。我們必須信賴他的判斷。）

★ rely on

We cannot rely on the weather.（我們不能靠天氣。）

★ trust

You cannot trust his memory too much.（你不能太相信他的記憶。）

★ dilly-dally 閒晃；遊手好閒

也可以這麼說 idle about

Jessie was advised not to idle about by her teacher.（潔西的老師建議她不要虛度光陰。）

★ to be a lazy good-for-nothing

Ken was a lazy good-for-nothing, but he has changed since his father died.（肯以前都遊手好閒，但他父親過世後他徹底地改變了。）

生活知識小補給

　　"A friend in need is a friend indeed." 是一句英文諺語，相對於中文的「患難見真情」，除了這一句與朋友有關的諺語外，還有幾句值得一提。"A true friend is known in the day of adversity." 一個真正的朋友是在逆境時，也就是中文的「患難見真情，疾風知勁草」。除了這一句，還有 "Misfortune tests the sincerity of friends." 厄運測試一個朋友的真誠，也就是類似「患難見真情」囉！

Unit 9

史瑞克三世
Up In Sb.'s Grill

動畫經典佳句

"Maybe I should cut him some slack."
也許我該饒了他。

"I am not trying to get up in your grill or raise your roof."
我不是故意要把你惹毛。

"Ladies, let go of your petty complaints and let's work together."
小姐們，不要再抱怨了，讓我們一起努力。

動畫內容敘述

Prince Charming and the other villains capture all of Shrek's fairy tale friends: Gingy, Pinocchio, the Big Bad Wolf, the Three Little Pigs, Dragon and Dronkeys. Fiona, Queen Lilian together with Doris, the Ugly Stepsister, Cinderella, Snow White, Sleeping Beauty and Rapunzel try to escape through an underground passage. However, Rapunzel betrays them and lead them to a trap. They discover that she is in love with Prince Charming, who plans to make her his queen after he becomes the King.

白馬王子及其他壞人抓住所有史瑞克的童話故事朋友：薑餅人、小木偶、大野狼、三隻小豬、龍和龍驢寶寶們。費歐娜、莉莉安皇后、桃樂絲、灰姑娘的醜姐姐、灰姑娘、白雪公主、睡美人及長髮公主試圖從一個地下通道逃離。然而，長髮公主卻背叛她們，將她們引入陷阱。她們發現長髮公主愛上白馬王子，他計畫成為國王後封長髮公主為皇后。

(參考網站：https://en.wikipedia.org/wiki/Shrek_the_Third)

Part 1
Part 2
Part 3
Part 4

 情境對話　Track 21

Wendy and Shannon joined a summer camp. When they arrived, they found out the facilities were not as good as they were told. They are unhappy about the arrangement made by travel agent, Andy.

Wendy:　Gee...there is no tap water here; we have to get water from that river.

Shannon: Well, this is called summer "camp", I guess. We need to experience the wild.

Wendy:　Are we going to take a shower in the river?

Shannon: I found out a hose from the toilet here.

Wendy:　Come on, it is so yucky. I am going to file up a complaint to Andy.

Shannon: Let go of your petty complaint and let's work together.

Wendy:　I am not gonna stay here for a minute. I will call Andy and ask him to pick me up. I am out of it.
　　　　(Wendy's cell phone is out of signal. A while later, she returns.)

Shannon: Will Andy come to pick you up?

Wendy:　Well, no signal in this far far away land. I am not trying to get up in your grill or raise your roof.

Shannon: I know. Maybe we should cut him some slack. What we need to do now is to sort out the problem and make ourselves more comfortable.

Wendy: I guess I have to take it.
Shannon: Ok! Let's put up our tent before it gets dark.

▸▸ 中譯

溫蒂及莎南參加一個夏令營。當她們到達時，發現設備和她們被告知的差很多。溫蒂很不高興旅行社安迪的安排。

溫蒂：天呀！這裡沒有水龍頭，我們要從河裡取水。

莎南：喔，大概是叫夏令「露營」吧！我們要體驗野外生活。

溫蒂：我們要在河裡洗澡嗎？

莎南：我發現有一條水管連接到廁所。

溫蒂：少來，好噁心。我要跟安迪抱怨。

莎南：不要再抱怨了，讓我們一起努力。

溫蒂：我絕不在這多留一分鐘。我要叫安迪來接我。我要走了。

　　　（溫蒂的手機沒訊號。一會兒之後，她回來。）

莎南：安迪會來接你嗎？

溫蒂：喔，在這遠得要命的地方，沒有訊號。我不是故意要把你惹毛。

莎南：我知道。也許我們該饒了他。我們要做的就是解決問題，讓我們
　　　自己舒服一點。

溫蒂：我想我得接受了。

莎南：好吧！在天黑前我們快搭帳棚。

單字片語解析

slack *n.* 鬆弛

Because of the slack in the factory, the supply cannot meet the demand.

因為工廠蕭條,供應無法符合需求。

grill *n.* 烤(肉)架

We need a grill to make barbecue.

我們做戶外烤肉需要烤肉架。

raise *v.* 舉起

The school needs to raise fund for a basketball team.

學校要設立籃球隊需要籌募基金。

你還可以這樣說

★ up in sb.'s grill 惹某人麻煩

也可以這麼說 someone's in your face

Jack's in your face, but you never mad at him. (傑克老是惹你麻煩,但你從未對他生氣。)

★ let go of 放開

也可以這麼說 lift the control over

He lifts the control over the leash to the dog. (他放開拴住狗的鍊子。)

★ cut someone some slack 饒了某人

也可以這麼說 give someone some slack

Give Jack some slack. He has suffered a lot.（饒了傑克，他已經受很多苦了。）

★ give someone a break

Give me a break. I need to be alone.（饒了我吧，我需要一人獨處。）

生活知識小補給

　　童話故事中的白馬王子都是善良、英俊、高大、有責任感，得以勝任一國之君的重責大任。你有沒有想過，如果白馬王子是個大壞蛋呢？對很多情竇初開的女孩來說，只要是愛她的人，都是白馬王子，於是身邊友人的勸告，父母的忠告，都成了刺耳的話語。等待熱戀回歸平淡，良人日漸成狼人，才驚覺自己的錯誤判斷。愛是盲目的，如何保護自己，也許只有多聽聽身邊人的建議，才能明辨白馬王子非黑馬王子。

1 Part

2 Part

3 Part

4 Part

Unit 10

鯊魚黑幫
Snap Up

"So you won't mind if I steal him for a while, will you?"

所以你不會介意我借他一下吧？

"Get a hold of yourself, man. This is no time to act crazy."

拜託你神經繃緊一點。我們沒時間莊孝維。

"Has the reef's most eligible bachelor been snapped up?"

珊瑚區最有身價的光棍死會了嗎？

動畫內容敘述

Oscar leaves Lola for Angie after Angie reveals that she had feelings for Oscar even before he became famous, but this leaves Lola determined to get revenge. Oscar buys some Valentine's Day gifts for Angie. Before he can present them to her, he finds that Don Lino has kidnapped Angie to force a sit-down. Lenny comes along now disguised as a dolphin named Sebastian. They arrive at the meeting to find Lola next to Don Lino, while Angie is tied up and gagged and presented to Don Lino on a plate who prepares to eat her if Oscar does not comply. Lenny grabs Angie into his mouth, but later regurgitates her.

在安姬告知奧斯卡她在他成名前就喜歡他了後，奧斯卡為了安姬離開蘿拉，卻引來蘿拉的報復。奧斯卡買情人節禮物給安姬，但送她之前，他發現湯大尾綁架安姬，要他坐下來談判。連尼跟著去，並偽裝成海豚賽巴斯汀。他們到達後，發現蘿拉在湯大尾身邊，安姬則被綁著放在盤子上，若奧斯卡不服從，她就準備被吃掉。連尼一把吃掉安姬，但之後卻反胃吐出她。

（參考網站：https://en.wikipedia.org/wiki/Shark_Tale）

1 Part

2 Part

3 Part

4 Part

 情境對話 Track 22

Tom, a CEO of a company, and John, a chief manager of the same company, are good friends. They are in the middle of a meeting, which discusses about the launching scheme of their new products. Suddenly, Caroline knocks the door. Gee, she is really a hot babe to Tom...

Caroline: You won't mind if I steal Tom for a while, will you? (Caroline left...)

John: Wake up, man. You are not gonna leave, right?

Tom: Isn't she a hot babe? If I go for a couple of minutes...

John: Get a hold of yourself, man. This is no time to act crazy.

Tom: Um...

John: We are in the middle of the important meeting. Just stay here for another hour or two, then, you will be free.

Tom: All right! Where were we?

John: Has the most eligible bachelor been snapped up?

Tom: Well, she is a smart and charming... coworker.

John: Come on. I have known you since college. Let's get our business done soon. OK?

▸▸ **中譯**

一家公司的執行長湯姆和同一家公司的總經理強，是好朋友。他們正在開會討論公司新產品的上市計畫中。突然，凱洛琳敲門進來。天呀，她對湯姆來說真是個辣妹……

凱洛琳：你不會介意我借湯姆一下吧？

　　　　（凱洛琳離開……）

約翰：　醒來，老兄。你不是要馬上離開吧？

湯姆：　她很辣，是吧？如果我出去一兩分鐘……

約翰：　拜託你神經繃緊一點。我們沒時間莊孝維。

湯姆：　嗯……

約翰：　我們正在重要會議中。在這待一或兩個小時，然後，你就自由了。

湯姆：　好吧！我們到哪裡了？

約翰：　我們最有身價的單身漢死會了嗎？

湯姆：　嗯，她是個很聰明且很迷人的……同事。

約翰：　少來了。大學時期我就認識你了。我們趕快把工作搞定。好嗎？

🎨 單字片語解析

🚩 **steal** *v.* 偷

The girl steals my heart at the first sight.

那女孩在第一眼就偷走了我的心（我戀愛了）。

🚩 **crazy** *adj.* 瘋狂的

The boy's crazy behavior irritates other kids.

那男孩的瘋狂行為讓很多孩子生氣。

🚩 **reef** *n.* 礁

The group of divers support "Clean the Reef" activity.

那一群潛水員支持「淨礁岩」活動。

🐘 你還可以這樣說

★ snap up 搶購；爭奪

也可以這麼說 shopping rush

Many people think only women like shopping rush.（很多人認為只有女人喜歡瘋狂搶購。）

★ panic buying

On hearing the news of typhoon, lots of people go on panic buying.（聽到颱風的消息，很多人跑去瘋狂搶購。）

★ fight for

The dragon boat teams should fight for the flag to win.（龍舟團隊要爭奪旗子以獲勝。）

★ struggle for

The mountain climbers struggle for their lives at K2.（在喬戈里峰（世界第二高峰）的登山者為他們的生命奮鬥。）

★ contest for

Geraldine enters the contest for Miss World.（嬌拉汀競選世界小姐。）

生活知識小補給

　　在兩性的世界中，男女追逐的遊戲分秒都在上演。溫柔平實的安姬和火辣美艷的蘿拉，因為吃醋，上演一場復仇之旅。男女感情常常因為處理不當而擦槍走火。在英文諺語中有一句 "The grass is (always) greener on the other side." 告訴我們「鄰家的草永遠比較綠」，也是一種人生的哲學，有人說「天涯何處無芳草」，是呀！你怎麼知道下一個人不會更好？一次次的經驗將協助你更聰明的選擇伴侶，找到更棒的，何必報仇，感恩都來不及呢！不是嗎？

1 Part

2 Part

3 Part

4 Part

Unit 11

海底總動員
Thanks, Mate.

動畫經典佳句

"Do you like to come to a little get-together I'm doing?"
你要不要來小聚一下？

"Thanks, mate. A little chum to chum, eh?"
謝了，老兄。朋友對朋友，是嗎？

"I am glad I got that off my chest."
我很高興我終於說出口了。

動畫內容敘述

Marlin meets Dory, a native and optimistic Regal Blue Tang with short-term memory loss, in search of help to find Nemo. He meets would-be vegetarian sharks: Bruce, Anchor and Chum and finds a diver mask dropped from the boat. Marlin notices an address written on it. When he argues with Dory and accidentally gives her a nosebleed, the blood scent causes Bruce to enter an uncontrollable feeding frenzy. The pair escape from Bruce but the mask falls into a trench in the deep sea. While struggling with an Angler Fish in the deep sea, Dory notes down the address on the mask as Sydney, Australia.

馬林在尋找尼莫的路上遇見一隻好心腸、樂觀，但有短暫失憶的藍唐王魚，多莉，幫助他一同尋找尼莫。他遇見宣誓成為素食主義的鯊魚：布魯斯、安哥、和瓊，並發現從船上掉落的潛水夫蛙鏡。馬林注意到上頭有寫著地址。當他和多莉吵架時，意外地讓她的鼻子流血，鮮血的氣味讓布魯斯失控，變成瘋狂嗜食的狀態。他們逃離布魯斯，但蛙鏡卻掉到深海海溝中。當在深海溝中和琵琶魚奮戰時，多莉記住蛙鏡上的住址是在澳洲雪梨。

(參考網站：http://disney.wikia.com/wiki/Finding_Nemo)

 情境對話 Track 23

Bartley broke up with his girlfriend. He is terribly upset. He turns off his cell phone, blocks his Facebook and cuts off his line. No one can reach him. His friends worry a lot. Jacob bumps into him on the street.

Jacob: How have you been? We are so worried about you.

Bartley: My nerve can't take much more of this.

Jacob: Relax. It's not the end of the world. Haven't you heard that "there are plenty more fish in the sea"?

Bartley: Look at you. I am home.

Jacob: Do you like to come to a little get-together I'm doing?

Bartley: Thanks, mate. A little chum to chum, eh?

Jacob: Right! We are still chums.

Bartley: I don't know that it has been really painful since she left.

Jacob: Come on, man. The sun is still shining out there.

Bartley: I am glad I got that off my chest. You are an inspiration.

Jacob: Well, better luck next time. Cheer up!

▶▶ **中譯**

巴特萊和女友分手。他非常沮喪。他關掉手機，關閉臉書，甚至將 Line 切斷。沒有人找得到他。他的朋友很擔心。杰考柏在街上突然遇見他。

杰考柏：你還好嗎？我們都很擔心你呢！

巴特萊：我的神經緊繃無法再承受更多。

杰考柏：放輕鬆，又不是世界末日。你沒聽說「天涯何處無芳草」嗎？

巴特萊：看到你，我很放鬆。

杰考柏：你要不要來小聚一下？

巴特萊：謝了，老兄。朋友對朋友，是嗎？

杰考柏：對呀！我們還是好朋友。

巴特萊：我不知她離開後會那麼痛。

杰考柏：好了，好傢伙。太陽還是一樣燦爛。

巴特萊：我很高興我終於說出口了。你真的很鼓舞。

杰考柏：嗯，下一個會更好。振作起來！

單字片語解析

little *adj.* 小的

The little boy cannot hold the glass.

那小男孩無法握住那個玻璃杯。

get-together *n.* 聚會

My family have a get-together party every week.

我的家人每星期有一次聚會。

mate *n.* 夥伴

You are the best mate that I've ever had.

你是我最好的夥伴。

你還可以這樣說

★ mate 夥伴；同伴

也可以這麼說 partner

Rebecca is an excellent partner.（麗貝嘉是個很棒的夥伴。）

★ companion

It is not very easy to find a good companion.（找一個好同伴不是一件很容易的事。）

★ fellow

Eric was requested to pick up his team fellows.（艾瑞克被要求揀選他自己團隊的夥伴。）

★ colleague

My colleagues are not very helpful.（我的同伴不是很有幫助。）

★ business associate

We need business associates to get the job done.（我們需要同伴將工作做好。）

生活知識小補給

人的大腦，一直是個神祕區域，很多部位科學家仍無法解開其作用的謎團。去年（2015 年）諾貝爾醫學獎，解開了人類海馬迴的謎，大腦的定位導航系統(GPS)的作用一旦受損，就失去定位記憶。短暫失憶(short-term memory loss)跟老年癡呆也有部分關聯。人類大腦會將記憶存在不同區域，分為短暫記憶區及長期記憶區。短暫記憶區大部分存在大腦的額葉，而短暫失憶，就是從 30 秒到幾天之久的記憶消失，一般缺氧、酒精或藥物濫用、癲癇及外傷都可能造成短暫記憶喪失。

1 Part

2 Part

3 Part

4 Part

Unit 12

超人特攻隊
Settle Down

動畫經典佳句

"Settle down? Are you kidding? I'm at the top of my game. I'm up there with the big dogs! Girl, come on."
定下來？你在開玩笑嗎？我的狀況這麼好，處於顛峰。女孩，別扯了。

"Doubt is a luxury we can't afford anymore, sweetie."
親愛的，懷疑是一種奢侈，我們再也負擔不起。

"You keep trying to pick a fight, but I'm just happy you're alive."
你一直想吵架，而我正高興著你還活著。

動畫內容敘述

Elastigirl Helen has become suspicious of Mr. Incredible Bob having an affair. Bob finds out a tear in his suit, he visits superhero costume designer Edna Mode who decides to make him and his whole family suits, each outfitted with a tracking device, unknown to Helen and the kids. Bob visits Nomanisan again and discovers that Mirage is working for Buddy Pine, a formerly overbearing super-fan rejected by him and now identifying as super-villain Syndrome. Helen triggers Bob's tracking device, identifying the remote island but inadvertently revealing Bob's presence to Syndrome and causing him to be captured.

彈力女超人海倫懷疑超能先生鮑勃有外遇。鮑勃發現他的衣服有破洞，於是找了製作超人衣的衣夫人，她決定幫他一家人做一套超人衣，而每一件衣服都有一個追蹤器，這件事海倫和孩子都不知。鮑勃到了諾曼島，發現幻影為他先前拒絕的瘋狂粉絲超勁先生工作，現在超勁先生成為大壞蛋辛拉登。海倫啟動鮑勃的追蹤器，發現他在遙遠的島嶼，卻因此不小心洩漏了鮑勃的行蹤，害他被辛拉登逮到。

(參考網站：http://disney.wikia.com/wiki/The_Incredibles)

1 Part

2 Part

3 Part

4 Part

 Track 24

Yuki has dated with Raymond for 5 years. She is expecting to be proposed. However, Raymond is often busy with his business. She is not sure if he is her Mr. Right. They are going to have a dinner to celebrate their anniversary tonight. Yuki will ask if he is still care about this relationship.

Yuki: Thank you, sweetie. It is a wonderful meal. Happy anniversary!

Raymond: As long as you are happy.

Yuki: How long have we been seen each other?

Raymond: Five years I guess.

Yuki: That's right. Honey, have you ever thought about settling down?

Raymond: Settle down? Are you kidding? I'm at the top of my game. I'm up there with the big dogs! Girl, come on.

Yuki: Are you seeing somebody?

Raymond: No, why? Doubt is a luxury we can't afford anymore, sweetie.

Yuki: You don't seem interested in marrying me.

Raymond: You keep trying to pick a fight, but I'm just happy you're alive.

Yuki: You do care about me?

Raymond: Certainly. I am too busy at work just want to promise you a better future.

Yuki:　　　I love you.
Raymond:Ditto.

▶ **中譯**

由希和雷蒙約會五年了。她在等雷蒙求婚。但是，雷蒙總是忙著工作。她不確定他是不是她的白馬王子。他們今晚要一起吃晚餐慶祝認識周年。由希將問雷蒙他是否在意這一段感情。

由希：謝謝你，親愛的。很棒的晚餐，周年快樂！

雷蒙：只要妳開心。

由希：我們認識多久了？

雷蒙：我猜五年。

由希：對呀，親愛的，你有想過要定下來嗎？

雷蒙：定下來？你在開玩笑嗎？我的狀況這麼好，處於顛峰。女孩，別扯了。

由希：你有在和別人約會嗎？

雷蒙：沒有，為什麼？懷疑是一種奢侈，我們負擔不起。

由希：你似乎沒有興趣跟我結婚。

雷蒙：你不斷想吵架，而我正高興著你還活著。

由希：你真的在乎我嗎？

雷蒙：當然。我太忙著工作，只是想承諾妳一個未來。

由希：我愛你。

雷蒙：我也是。

單字片語解析

settle down *ph.* 定下來

Mary doesn't want to settle down before she gets a PhD degree.

瑪莉不想在拿到博士學位之前定下來。

kid *v.* 開玩笑

It is not kidding that the earthquake will happen soon.

地震近期內會發生不是開玩笑的。

doubt *v.* 懷疑

The trick the magician performed is still a doubt.

那魔術師表演的魔術讓人很疑惑。

你還可以這樣說

★ pick a fight 吵架；爭吵

也可以這樣說 quarrel

The couple living next door quarrels all the time. （住隔壁的那一對夫婦總是在吵架。）

★ fall out

These kids fall out for their toys. （這些孩子為他們的玩具爭吵。）

★ make a scene

Two women made a scene at a traditional market because of a bunch of vegetables.（兩個女人在傳統市場因為一把菜吵架。）

★ argue

The two injured riders argued at the spot of traffic accident.（兩個受傷騎士在車禍地點吵架。）

★ be at odds with somebody

The old lady is at odd with everyone in the neighborhood.（那老女人跟每個鄰居吵架。）

生活知識小補給

衣服材質輕柔、保暖又容易乾，一直是科學家想研發的，近年仿生學的盛行，科學家從蜘蛛絲中找到許多靈感。蜘蛛絲，我們已知它是目前生物界中最具韌性之蛋白質纖維，由數十至數百根微絲抱合而成絲，兼具輕量、柔軟、彈性、生物可分解和自我組裝修補等特性。蜘蛛絲的主要成分為蛋白質胺基酸，也有某些蜘蛛絲化學成分多達 300 種以上，非常的複雜，科學家曾將蜘蛛基因轉殖在羊奶中，仍無法以人工方式加以完全合成仿製。

3
Part

學校工作

冰雪奇緣
You Must Learn to Control.

👑 動畫經典佳句

"Your power will grow. There is beauty in it, but also great dangerous."
你的力量將會茁壯。裡面存在著美麗，但也非常的危險。

"You must learn to control. Fear will be your enemy."
你必須學會控制。恐懼將會是你的敵人。

"I am a victim of fear. I've been traumatized."
我是恐懼的受害者，我已經受創傷了。

動畫內容敍述

The princesses, Elsa and Anna, of Arendelle play with Olaf, until Anna makes a leap as Elsa slips on the ice. The blast of power means to create a pile of snow, but hits Anna in the head, knocking her unconscious. Their parents hastily load their daughters onto their horses and ride at full speed into the mountains. The girls' parents ask the boulders for help. The leader of the trolls, Pabbie, shows up and asks the King if Elsa is born or cursed with her abilities. Pabbie warns Elsa that her powers would grow, and although they are beautiful, they will be dangerous if she could not learn to control them, as fear would be her greatest enemy.

Arendelle 的兩個公主，艾莎和安娜在與雪寶玩耍時，安娜跳躍，艾莎滑倒在冰上，她原本使出的冰凍力量是要弄一座冰山，卻不慎打到安娜的頭，讓她頓時失去知覺。她們的父母緊急將她們放在馬車上，全速帶到山裡尋求石精靈的協助。長老佩比問國王，艾莎是否因詛咒而出生。佩比警告艾莎，她的能力將不斷增強，雖然它們是如此的美麗，卻也極為危險，若她無法學會控制它們，那恐懼將會是她最強大的敵人。

（參考網站：*http://disney.wikia.com/wiki/Frozen*）

1 Part

2 Part

3 Part

4 Part

 Track 25

George is a nine-year-old boy. He can see ghosts. He is scared. His grandmother is a wise woman. She finds out that George has the same ability as she does. She tries to comfort him and tell him about his magic power.

Granny: Hi, my dear, what are you afraid of?

George: I am so scared that I often see those ugly people around me, but mother cannot see them.

Granny: Wow, so cool, you have the magic power.

George: No, I don't wanna see them. They look terrible.

Granny: You know what? You are the guardian angel to them. You are the one who can help them, because you can see them.

George: Really?

Granny: Yes, your power will grow. There is beauty in it, but it's also very dangerous. You must learn to control it. If you don't, fear will be your enemy.

George: I am a victim of fear. I've been traumatized.

Granny: You should learn to have control over your power. You will find out you are a gift from god.

▶▶ 中譯

喬治是個九歲的孩子。他看得見鬼魂。他很害怕。他的奶奶是個有智慧的女人。她發現喬治跟她一樣有著相同的能力。她試著安撫並告訴他有關他的神奇能力。

奶奶：嘿，親愛的，你害怕甚麼？

喬治：我好怕，我常看到我身邊有一些很醜的人，但是媽媽都看不見。

奶奶：哇，好棒，你有神奇能力。

喬治：不，我不想看到他們，他們看起來好恐怖。

奶奶：你知道嗎？你是他們的守護天使，你是可以幫助他們的人，因為你可以看見他們。

喬治：真的嗎？

奶奶：是的，你的力量將會茁壯。裡面存在著美麗，但也非常的危險。你必須學會控制。如果你不學，恐懼將會是你的敵人。

喬治：我是恐懼的受害者，我已經受創傷了。

奶奶：你必須學會控制你的能力，你會發現你是上帝給予的珍貴禮物。

單字片語解析

power *n.* 能力

She has the power to change the world.

她有改變這個世界的能力。

control *v.* 控制

You should learn how to control the machine.

你應該學習如何控制這個機器。

enemy *n.* 敵人

We should not be afraid of enemy.

我們不應該害怕敵人。

你還可以這樣說

★ must 必須

你也可以這麼說 have to

You have to study hard. （你必須認真讀書。）

★ ought to

You ought to take the responsibility. （你必須負責任。）

★ will 將

你也可以這麼說 be going to

Nancy is going to take the course.（南茜將修這一堂課。）

★ be about to

The train is about to depart.（火車將要啟程。）

★ be to

You are to choose the right answer.（你將選擇正確答案。）

🦋 生活知識小補給

　　當我們擁有與別人不一樣的天賦或長相，常常會不知所措。筆者曾有一位亞斯柏格症的學生，他因為一些行為與無法自我控制的特性，讓自己有一段時間非常沮喪，並自暴自棄。他在機械方面是非常特出的，但在人際關係上，卻是讓他苦惱不已。經過一陣子與他深刻的對談後，他慢慢理解他的天賦，接受自己，並努力以自我的長處彌補不足。每一個人，都是上天給予的最美好的禮物，接受自己，才能突破自我。你是否了解自己，正在尋求突破呢？

1 Part

2 Part

3 Part

4 Part

腦筋急轉彎
Leave Me Alone.

👑 動畫經典佳句

"So, Riley, how was your first day at school?"

"Fine, I guess. I don't know."

所以，萊莉，你第一天上學如何？

好，我猜，我不知道。

"Riley, I do not like this new attitude."

"What is your problem? Just leave me alone."

萊莉，我不喜歡這個新的態度。

你有甚麼問題？不要管我。

"Listen, young lady, I don't know where this respect-ful attitude came from."

聽好，女孩，我不知道這個令人尊敬的態度是哪來的。

動畫內容敘述

Riley and her parents sit around the dinner table eating Chinese takeout. Riley's in a bad mood, her parents are trying to figure out what's going wrong. We can clearly see how the emotions inside all three minds react. Riley's mother sees her upset, and she's upset by it, but not in the sense of being angry. She's noticing the stress on Riley. She probably feels a bit "helpless" to do anything about it. Dad is clearly stressed out about the move. Finally, he is irritated by Riley's attitude. Obviously, he couldn't sense her emotion and shows his empathy.

萊莉和她的父母坐在餐桌旁吃中國外賣食物。萊莉心情很不好,她的父母試著找出到底發生了甚麼事。我們可以清楚看到三個人的內心情緒是如何反應的。萊莉的媽媽清楚見到她的沮喪,她也因此很沮喪,但沒有看見生氣的感覺。她注意到萊莉的壓力,她可能覺得有一點「無助」。而父親,明顯地很緊張。最後,他被萊莉的態度激怒。很顯然地,他無法感知到萊莉的情感並發揮同理心。

(參考網站:http://disney.wikia.com/wiki/The_Disney_Wiki)

情境對話 Track 26

Joe just got a new job. He was so excited. Unfortunately, he had a bad day. He decided to go to the company earlier, but the traffic was very bad. At the end, he was late for half an hour. After he got off work, he found out his car was towed away. He felt so upset when he got home.

Dad: Joe, how was your first day at work?

Joe: Fine, I guess. I don't know.

Dad: What happened? Don't you like your new job? How about your new boss? You told me everything is gonna be great, didn't you? How is your office? What did you do for the whole day? How is your car?

Joe: Dad, stop it. Could you just please shut up?

Dad: Well, I do not like this new attitude.

Joe: What is your problem? Just leave me alone.

Dad: Listen, young boy, I don't know where this respectful attitude came from. Go back to your room.

Joe: (slam the door and left)...

▶▶ 中譯

喬伊有新工作了。他很開心。很不幸地,這一天真是糟透了。他決定早一點到公司,但是交通阻塞得很嚴重。最後,竟遲到半小時。下班時,他發現汽車被拖吊了。他回家時覺得超沮喪。

爸爸:喬伊,第一天工作如何呀?

喬伊:好,我猜,我不知道。

爸爸:發生甚麼事?你不喜歡你的新工作嗎?你的新老闆如何?你跟我說一切會很好的,不是嗎?你的辦公室如何呀?你一整天都在做甚麼?你的車如何呀?

喬伊:爸,停,你可不可以閉嘴?

爸爸:啊!我不喜歡這個新的態度。

喬伊:你有甚麼問題?不要管我。

爸爸:聽好,年輕人,我不知道這個令人尊敬的態度來自哪裡。回你房間去。

喬伊:(摔了門離開)…

單字片語解析

guess *v.* 推測

I can guess what will happen tomorrow.

我可以猜猜明天會發生甚麼事。

attitude *n.* 態度

Attitude decides your latitude.

態度決定你的高度。

problem *n.* 問題

He is good at solving problems.

他很會解決問題。

你還可以這樣說

★ leave me alone 不要管我

也可以這麼說 let me alone

Don't say anything. Let me alone.（不要說甚麼，不要管我。）

★ stay away from me

Please stay away from me.（不要管我（離我遠一點）。）

★ guess 猜測

也可以這麼說 speculate

She speculates that tomorrow will rain.（她猜測明天會下雨。）

★ to give a guess

She cannot finish all the questions, so she decides to give a guess.（她無法完成所有問題，所以她決定猜答案。）

★ to make a guess at

We make a guess at the riddle.（我們猜謎語。）

生活知識小補給

　　情緒是人的一部分，人的大腦，分為左腦和右腦，左腦掌管邏輯、數學等理性的範疇，右腦則是掌管圖案和想像力等感性直覺的部分。我們必須左右腦都要照顧到，但是卻常常忽略感性的右腦，只重視理性的左腦。情緒管理在今天的社會中，顯得極其重要。對負面的情緒，我們該學習的不是壓抑它，而是學習如何在不傷害別人及自己的前提下，學習抒發情緒，也許可以利用轉移注意力或運動的方式來達到更健康的身心靈。

Unit 3

怪獸大學
Partner Up.

👑 動畫經典佳句

"Okay, everyone, partner up, get your field trip buddy!"

好，各位，找夥伴，去戶外教學囉！

"Come on. It's a fraternity and sorority party. We have to go!"

來啦，麥可，這是兄弟會跟姊妹會的派對，我們一定要去！

"Enjoy the attention while it lasts, boys."

在活動中請專心，男孩們。

🛸 動畫內容敘述

During a field trip to the Monsters Inc factory, the friendless 6-year-old Mike Wazowski is forced to walk with his teacher Karen Graves. When the class visits the Scare Floor, they meet Superstar Scarer, Frank McCay, telling them he studied Scaring by going to Monsters University. Frank says that Monsters University is really the better school. As soon as Frank enters the child's room, Mike follows and secretly looks at Frank sneaking to the bed and avoiding the child's parents by pretending to be a piece of clothing. When the parents go away, Frank sneaks up to the child and scares him.

到怪獸電力公司的戶外教學，沒有朋友的麥可被迫跟他的老師凱倫‧格雷夫斯走在一起。當班上走到驚嚇樓層，他們見到超級驚嚇明星法蘭克‧麥凱，告訴他們他在怪獸大學修讀驚嚇學。他說怪獸大學真的是一所比較好的學校。當法蘭克進入小孩房間，麥可跟著，並悄悄地看著法蘭克偷偷摸摸爬到床上，假裝成一塊布避開孩子的父母。當孩子的父母離開後，他就爬起來嚇他。

（參考網站：http://disney.wikia.com/wiki/Monsters_University）

1 Part

2 Part

3 Part

4 Part

 情境對話 Track 27

Jerry and Hans are classmates. They go on a field trip to a university. Jerry and Hans are paired up by their teacher. They have a chat on the bus. They all feel so excited.

Teacher: Okay, everyone, partner up, get your field trip buddy!

Jerry: Wow, cool, today is gonna be great. Look at the sun, beautiful!

Hans: I have chewing gum. Would you like to have some?

Jerry: Cool, man. Will you come to the party tomorrow?

Hans: What party? I will have to finish the math homework tomorrow.

Jerry: It's a fraternity and sorority party. We have to go!

Hans: I really need to stay in the library tomorrow.

Jerry: Come on. They invite NBA player, Michael Jordan, to the party. It will be awesome.

Hans: Really? He is my idol. You are not kidding, right?

Teacher: Enjoy the attention while it lasts, boys.

Jerry: (whisper) No, man! You got to be there.

Hans: How exciting. I will. Thanks, mate!

▸▸ 中譯

杰瑞和漢斯是同學。他們到一所大學戶外教學。杰瑞和漢斯被老師分在同一組。他們在巴士上聊天。同學們都覺得好興奮。

老師：好，各位，找夥伴，去戶外教學囉！

杰瑞：哇，讚，今天一定很棒，看太陽，真好！

漢斯：我有口香糖。你要嗎？

杰瑞：好呀，老兄。你明天要去派對嗎？

漢斯：甚麼派對？我明天要完成數學功課。

杰瑞：這是兄弟會跟姊妹會的派對，我們一定要去！

漢斯：我明天真的要在圖書館。

杰瑞：來啦。他們邀請 NBA 球星麥可喬頓到派對來，一定會超讚。

漢斯：真的嗎？他是我的偶像。你沒開我玩笑吧？

老師：在活動中請專心，男孩們。

杰瑞：（輕聲）沒，老兄，你一定要去啦！

漢斯：太興奮了，我一定會，謝了，夥伴！

單字片語解析

partner *v.* 合夥

Gary partnered with John at the project.

杰瑞和強合夥做計劃。

field *n.* 田野；實地

We need to do field study twice this semester.

這學期我們要做兩次田野調查。

fraternity *n.* 大學兄弟會

Boys are members of fraternity in the university.

在大學，男孩都是兄弟會的一員。

sorority *n.* 大學姐妹會

Tiffany is the leader of sorority.

蒂芬妮是大學姊妹會的會長。

attention *n.* 注意

May I have your attention, please?

麻煩可以注意我這邊嗎？

last *v.* 度過

He is very sick. I am afraid he will not last tonight.

他病得很嚴重，我很擔心他度不過今晚。

你還可以這樣說

★ partner up 找夥伴

也可以這樣說 pair up

We were asked to pair up for the activity.（我們在活動中被要求配對。）

★ enjoy the attention 專心

也可以這樣說 pay attention

Teacher asks us to pay attention in the class.（老師要求我們在課堂上要專心。）

★ listen up

Listen up! I have an announcement to make.（注意聽！我要宣布一件事。）

生活知識小補給

　　在國外大學院校的兄弟會或姊妹會，大概有五個組成要素：(1) 秘密；(2) 單一性別會員；(3) 新會員需要宣誓；(4) 占用大學會員住宿地方做為會址；(5) 使用一組複雜的東西，像是希臘字、徽章、密碼…等做為辨識記號。兄弟會或姊妹會參與學校慈善活動，並常訓練新會員，像是教導禮儀、衣著、禮貌、建立網絡及為畢業生創造就業機會。

Unit 4

食破天驚 2
I Won't Tell A Soul.

👑 **動畫經典佳句**

"Sir, I won't tell a soul."
先生，我不會告訴別人。

"Wait a second, he is buffering."
等一下，他在緩衝一下。

"You are going to join me and help us make the world a better place."
你將會加入我並將世界變成一個更好的地方。

動畫內容敘述

Inventor Flint Lockwood's genius is finally being recognized as he's invited by his idol Chester V to join The Live Corp Company, where the best and brightest inventors in the world create technologies for the betterment of mankind. It's always been Flint's dream to be recognized as a great inventor, but everything changes when he discovers that his most infamous machine (which turns water into food) is still operating and is now creating food-animal hybrids-"foodimals!" With the fate of humanity in his hands, Chester sends Flint and his friends on a dangerously delicious mission- to battle hungry tacodiles, shrimpanzees, hippotatomuses, cheespiders and other food creatures to save the world again!

發明家富林天才，最後被他的偶像阿奇師，邀請到創造科技，一家擁有全世界最好、最棒的發明家，以發明讓人類過得更好的公司工作。被認同為偉大的發明家，一直是富林的夢想。但當他發現他聲名狼藉的機器（能把水變成食物）還在運作，而現在還製造出雜種食物動物時，卻改變了每件事。阿奇師給富林及他的朋友一項危險又好吃的任務—對抗饑餓的塔克鱷魚、蝦猩猩、馬鈴薯河馬、起司蜘蛛及其他食物生物，以再度拯救世界。

（參考網站：https://en.wikipedia.org/wiki/Cloudy_with_a_Chance_of_Meatballs_2）

1
Part

2
Part

3
Part

4
Part

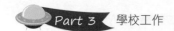

Leon has a friend, Tom, who likes to assemble parts at his father's garage alone. One day, he invited Leon to visit his secret garage and told him that he invented a flying robot. Leon is very excited.

(In front of the garage)

Tom: You are my good friend, but promise me not to tell anybody just now.

Leon: I won't tell a soul. I promise.

(Tom opens the door.)

Tom: Look at this.

Leon: Wow, it's amazing. But, how does it work?

Tom: The power is here.

Leon: Why can't it move?

Tom: Wait a second. It is buffering.

Leon: How come it's so small?

Tom: It's a personal robot. It can fly you to anywhere without worrying about the parking problem. You are going to join me and help us make the world a better place.

Leon: How can I help?

Tom: You are the expert in electricity. I need your help to get this job done.

Leon: Cool, man. I am in.

Tom: All right. Let's get started.

▶▶ 中譯

里昂有一個朋友,湯姆,喜歡在他爸爸的車庫裡獨自組裝零件。一天,他邀請里昂去他的祕密車庫,並告訴他,他發明了一個飛行機器人。里昂非常興奮。

（在車庫前）

湯姆:　你是我的好朋友,但答應我現在不能告訴任何人。

里昂:　我發誓,我不會告訴別人。

　　　　（湯姆打開門。）

湯姆:　看這個。

里昂:　哇,太驚人了。但是,它怎麼運作呀?

湯姆:　電開關在這。

里昂:　為什麼不能動?

湯姆:　等一下,它在緩衝。

里昂:　為什麼這麼小?

湯姆:　這是個人機器人。他可以帶你飛到任何地方,不必擔心停車問題。你將會加入我,把世界變成一個更好的地方。

里昂:　我能幫甚麼?

湯姆:　你是電的專家,我需要你幫我把這件事處理好。

里昂:　太棒了,老兄。我加入。

湯姆:　好,讓我們開始吧!

1
Part

2
Part

3
Part

4
Part

單字片語解析

soul *n.* 靈魂

Brevity is the soul of wit.

簡潔是智慧的靈魂。

wait *v.* 等待

Time waits for no one.

時光不待人。

second *n.* 秒

This clock is only few seconds late.

這個時鐘只晚了約幾秒。

你還可以這樣說

★ tell a soul 告訴別人

也可以這樣說 tell someone

Please tell someone who cares about the world.

（請告訴關心世界的人。）

★ tell anybody

I will not tell anybody about what happened.

（我不會告訴別人發生甚麼事。）

★ Wait a second. 等一下

也可以這樣說 Just a moment.

Just a moment, I will fix up soon.

（等一下，我會盡快修好。）

★ Just a minute.

Just a minute. The boss will be here soon.

（等一下，老闆馬上來。）

★ Please wait.

Please wait. She will be right here.

（請等一下，她馬上來）。

生活知識小補給

　　根據斯德哥爾摩國際水研究中心(SIWI)研究人員 Malik Falkemark 和其團隊所進行的研究報告指出：「如果我們按照目前西方國家的飲食趨勢推估變化，到了 2050 年，將不會有足夠的水源來灌溉農田，來餵飽 90 億的人口。」科學家表示，在越來越不穩定的氣候狀態下，調整飲食習慣是增加水資源的選項之一。因為動物性蛋白的食物來源，比植物性蛋白的食物來源，多消耗 5-10 倍的水資源，而全球有三分之一的農地種植了動物飼料呢！

Unit 5

羅雷司
Hush Your Mouth.

動畫經典佳句

"Hush your mouth. I was just trying to motivate you."
閉上你的嘴，我只是試著要啟發你。

"Plant the seed in the middle of town, where everyone can see. Change the way things are."
把種子種在城市的中間，每個人都可以看見，改變現狀。

"You can't reap what you don't sow."
你不耕種你就無法收穫。

動畫內容敘述

Ted is inspired by the Once-ler's gift of the last Truffula Seed to plant it to remind his town of the importance of nature. Ted is undeterred and enlists his family and Audrey to help plant the seed. Unfortunately, their attempt to plant the seed is interrupted by O'Hare who rallies the population to stop them. To convince them, Ted takes an earthmover and rams down a section of the city wall to reveal the environmental destruction outside. Shocked by the sight and inspired by Ted's conviction, the crowd defies O'Hare and the seed is planted.

泰迪受到萬事樂最後一棵松露樹的鼓舞，要將它種在他的城市以提醒自然的重要。泰迪毫不畏懼，召集他的家人及奧德莉幫忙種樹。很不幸地，他們試圖種樹的行為被歐海爾聚眾阻止。為了說服大家，泰迪用推土機撞倒城市一部分的牆，看到外頭被破壞的環境。人們被這樣的景致嚇到，就被泰迪說服了，並群起抗議歐海爾，於是種子終於被種了下去。

（參考網站：https://en.wikipedia.org/wiki/The_Lorax）

1
Part

2
Part

3
Part

4
Part

 情境對話 Track 29

Jerry is the boy who doesn't really care about the environment. He throws out garbage on the street. One day, he was just about to throw a sandwich wrapping paper on the ground. A wise old man approached him and stopped him from littering.

Old man: You know, when you blink, there are 74 trees chopped down. The forest which equals to the area of 20 tennis courts has disappeared.

Jerry: So? I did not do anything. I just try to throw out the garbage to the trash can.

Old man: Hush your mouth. I was just trying to motivate you. Take this magic seed.

Jerry: What should I do with it?

Old man: Plant the magic seed in the middle of the town, where everyone can see it. Change the way things are.
(Jerry did what he was told. Few months have gone by.)

Jerry: Wow, it's amazing. It is very joyful to see its budding.

Old man: What did you learn from this?

Jerry: It is not very easy to plant a tree. Even though plant cannot move, it is still a form of life.

Old man: You can't reap what you don't sow.

Jerry: Thank you. What a wonderful lesson you gave me!

▶▶ 中譯

杰瑞是個不關心環境的男孩。他把垃圾丟在街上。一天，他正要丟一個三明治紙包裝在地上時，一個老智者走向他並制止他亂丟垃圾。

老人：你知道嗎，當你一眨眼間，74 棵樹就被砍倒。相當於 20 個網球場大的森林就消失了。

杰瑞：所以呢？我沒做甚麼呀！我只是要把垃圾丟到垃圾桶。

老人：閉上你的嘴，我只是試著要啟發你。拿著這一顆神奇種子。

杰瑞：我要這顆種子做甚麼？

老人：把種子種在城市的中間，種在每個人都可以看見的地方，改變現狀。

（杰瑞照著老人的話做。幾個月後。）

杰瑞：哇，太神奇了。看到它發芽真的很開心。

老人：你從中學到了甚麼？

杰瑞：種一棵樹真的很不容易。即使樹不能動，它也是一個生命的型態。

老人：你不耕種你就無法收穫。

杰瑞：謝謝您。您給我上了一堂很棒的課！

Part 1

Part 2

Part 3

Part 4

單字片語解析

🚩 **hush** *v.* 使安靜

The teacher hushed the noisy students with music.

老師用音樂讓吵鬧的學生安靜下來。

🚩 **motivate** *v.* 給…動機

The sight of the scene motivates him.

看見那一幕引起了他的動機。

🚩 **middle** *adj.* 中間的

I was in the middle of work when he came.

他來的時候我正在工作。

🚩 **plant** *v.* 動詞

We planted many trees in the opening ceremony.

我們在開幕式時種了很多樹。

🚩 **reap** *v.* 收穫

If you try harder, you shall reap in joy.

如果你努力一點，你將會欣喜收穫。

🚩 **sow** *v.* 播種

The gardener sowed the yard with rose.

那園丁在後院種玫瑰。

你還可以這樣說

★ hush your mouth 閉上你的嘴
也可以這麼說 shut up
Can you please shut up?（可以請你閉嘴嗎？）

★ be quiet
Be quiet. The baby is sleeping!（安靜，嬰兒正在睡覺！）

★ You can't reap what you don't sow. 你不耕耘，你就無法收穫。
也可以這麼說 As you sow, so shall you reap.（一分耕耘一分收穫。）

★ No pain, no gain.（沒有付出就沒有收穫。）

生活知識小補給

　　過去 30 年來，世界肉品產量大約以 5% 的年增率成長，主要的增產是在開發中國家，約增加了三倍。儘管工業化國家的人均食肉量為開發中國家人民的三到四倍，但是開發中國家目前的產食量已超過世界肉品總量的一半，尤其是中國在過去 20 年來增加了一倍以上的消耗量。台灣人愛吃肉，每年每人食用畜產肉品約 77 公斤。少吃肉、騎單車、少消費是阻止地球快速暖化的重要法門。

1 Part

2 Part

3 Part

4 Part

Unit 6

史瑞克三世
Next In Line

👑 動畫經典佳句

"You weren't really next in line for the throne."
你不是下一位王位繼承人。

"The winds of fate have blown my destiny."
是命運的風要把我吹走。

"I will restore dignity to my throne."
我會重建我權勢的威嚴。

動畫內容敘述

Shrek tells Artie that he is the new king of Far Far Away at the school pep rally. Encouraged by his new title, Artie delivers a heart-felt speech, berating all the high school students and professing his undying love to Guinevere. Later, on board Shrek's ship, he is too excited to be on his way to the throne, until Donkey and Puss scare him by talking about the responsibilities of being a king. Artie changes his mind and wishes to return. He takes control of the ship, but ends up crashing it on an island where they meet Artie's wizard teacher, Mr. Merlin, who helps them to go back to the kingdom.

史瑞克在學校鼓舞士氣的集會上告訴亞帝，他是遠的要命王國的新國王。被他的新頭銜所鼓舞，他做了一個演講，嚴厲譴責高中同學並向吉薇兒表達愛意。之後，上了船，他太興奮即將即位的事，直到驢子和靴貓說到當國王該負的責任。亞帝改變主意想回去，他要控制船卻意外地把船撞毀。他們漂到一個島嶼，在那碰到他的巫師老師梅林，把他們送回王國。

（參考網站：*https://en.wikipedia.org/wiki/Shrek_the_Third*）

Part 1

Part 2

Part 3

Part 4

情境對話　Track 30

Mike is ambitious. He wants to join the campaign for the leader of student club. His buddy, David, does not like him to do so. He worries once he is elected, he won't hang out with him anymore. However, Mike needs his buddy to support him.

Mike: I really need your support. If you cannot stand by me, I will be very disappointed.

David: You weren't really next in line for the throne.

Mike: Why do you say so? You don't think I am qualified.

David: Not like that. I guess I am just a little bit selfish.

Mike: What do you mean by that? I have the feeling that the winds of fate have blown my destiny.

David: I am afraid you will not be my buddy anymore if you take the throne.

Mike: Don't you worry. I am your buddy forever. You got to help me.

David: Can I have your promise?

Mike: You bet. I will restore dignity to my throne.

David: Then, we have to draw up an effective strategy.

▶▶ 中譯

麥可很有野心。他想競選學生社團的會長。他的死黨，大衛，不喜歡他這麼做。他擔心他當上會長，就不會再跟他出去玩。可是，麥可需要他的死黨的支持。

麥可：我真的很需要你的支持。如果你無法挺我，我會很失望。

大衛：你不會是下一位會長。

麥可：你為何這麼說？你不認為我有資格。

大衛：也不是啦！我想我只是有一點自私。

麥可：你甚麼意思？我感覺是命運的風要把我吹走。

大衛：我擔心如果你當上會長，就不會再是我的死黨了。

麥可：別擔心，我們永遠都是死黨。你一定要幫我。

大衛：你會守住承諾嗎？

麥可：一定。我要重建我的威嚴。

大衛：那，我們要擬定一個有效的策略。

單字片語解析

line *n.* 隊伍

Please do not cut in line.

請不要插隊。

throne *n.* 王座

Sincerity is the key to the throne.

真誠是取得王位的關鍵。

fate *n.* 命運

The fate of the passengers on board is still unknown.

登機旅客的生死仍未卜。

你還可以這樣說

★ next in line 下一位；繼位

也可以這樣說 succeed to the throne

Jill succeeded to the throne of her father's business. （吉兒繼承她父親的事業。）

★ restore 恢復

也可以這樣說 recover

Lilian recovers from illness very soon. （莉莉安生病很快的復原了。）

★ regain

The business man soon regains his reputation.（那生意人很快回復他的聲譽。）

★ revive

The fish revive in the sea.（魚群在大海回復生機。）

★ return to

It took about three months for her to return to normal after the operation.（開刀後，花了她約三個月回復正常生活。）

生活知識小補給

　　當亞帝聽到自己要當國王的驚喜與自豪，讓他原本膽小無擔當的個性，突然之間膨脹到極點。後來，聽到原來國王要負很多責任，膽小的個性又讓他縮回原點。在職場上，我們也常常犯上這樣的毛病，當自己是小職員時，總是想望經理、總裁的位置，認為所有的吃香喝辣，榮華富貴都是他們獨享，很少人想到，真正坐上那一個王位時，所要承擔的重責大任，沒有能力的養成及經年累月的經驗，很難勝任而獲得民心的。成為一個好的領導，並不是一件容易的事呀！

史瑞克三世
The Only Person Standing In Your Way Is You.

動畫經典佳句

"Don't just because people treat you like a villain, or an ogre, or just some loser...doesn't mean you are one."

別因為別人把你像惡棍，或妖怪或是失敗者對待，並不代表你就是這樣的人。

"What matter most is what you think of yourself."

最重要的是你認為你自己是甚麼。

"If there's something you really want, or someone you want to be...the only person standing in your way is you."

如果你真的想做甚麼，或是想成為甚麼樣的人，唯一阻撓你的人就是你自己。

🛸 動畫內容敘述

Shrek, Donkey and Puss, the trios arrive to Worcestershire Academy, an elite boarding school. They discover that Arthur is a scrawny 16-year-old underachiever picked on by almost everyone. Far removed from the courageous legend his name evokes. Artie stands at the bottom of the high school food chain. He is constantly used as a punching bag by the school Jousting Team, led by the obnoxious Sir Lancelot and cruelly scorned by Guinevere who is the Valley Girl-like school "Queen Bee". These don't stop Shrek from persuading Artie to be next in line to the throne. In contrast, he believes he will be a very good king in the future.

史瑞克、驢子和靴貓三個到達菁英寄宿溫斯特秀學院。他們發現 16 歲瘦弱的亞瑟，是個被每個人欺負且成績不佳的人。跟他的偉大傳奇名字亞瑟，一點都不配。亞帝是學校食物鏈最底層的一個。他常常成為由藍斯勒閣下所領導的學校騎馬刺劍隊練習用的沙包，也被學校的「女王蜂」吉薇兒無情地諷刺。這些並無法阻止史瑞克說服亞帝回去繼任王位。相反的，他還認為他會成為一個很好的國王。

（參考網站：https://en.wikipedia.org/wiki/Shrek_the_Third）

1 Part

2 Part

3 Part

4 Part

 情境對話　Track 31

Sky is a new staff. He is shy and has no confidence. However, he is like an apple of his boss's eyes. His boss, William, believes he is a very talented boy, and he will be very successful if he can conquer his drawback.

William: Hi, Sky, come on in. Have a seat.

Sky: Hi, thank you.

William: So, tell me, how have you been these days at work?

Sky: I'm ok. I don't know if I can do better.

William: What about your coworkers? Do they offer any help?

Sky: Well, they think I am a freak.

William: Don't just because people treat you like a villain, or an ogre, or just some loser...doesn't mean you are one.

Sky: I guess I'm too shy to express myself.

William: What matters most is what you think of yourself.

Sky: I don't think I am good.

William: If there's something you really want, or someone you want to be...the only person standing in your way is you. Remember, you are a diamond to me.

Sky: Really? I will try my best, then. Thank you.

▶▶ 中譯

思凱是個新職員。他很害羞且沒自信。然而，他卻是老闆眼中的寶。他的老闆，威廉，相信他非常有天分，如果他能克服他的缺點，將來一定很有成就。

威廉：嗨，思凱，進來，坐下。

思凱：嗨，謝謝。

威廉：好，告訴我，這幾天工作如何？

思凱：我還好。我不知道我是不是能做得更好。

威廉：你的同事呢？他們提供協助嗎？

思凱：嗯，他們覺得我像個怪胎。

威廉：別因為別人把你像惡棍，或妖怪或是失敗者對待，並不代表你就是這樣的人。

思凱：我想我是太害羞而不敢表達我自己。

威廉：最重要的是你認為你自己是甚麼樣的人。

思凱：我不認為我很好。

威廉：如果你真的想做甚麼，或是想成為甚麼樣的人，唯一阻撓你的人就是你自己。記住，你對我來說像是一顆鑽石。

思凱：真的嗎？我會盡力做好。謝謝您。

單字片語解析

villain *n.* 惡棍

Paul acted as a villain in the science fiction movie.

保羅在那部科幻電影中演一名惡棍。

ogre *n.* 怪物

According to folklore, an ogre likes to eat human being.

根據民間傳說，怪物喜歡吃人類。

loser *n.* 失敗者

No one likes to be called a loser.

沒人喜歡被叫「魯蛇」（失敗者）。

你還可以這樣說

★ in one's way 妨礙某人

也可以這麼說 obstruct

The sign obstructing the traffic is very dangerous.（那妨礙到交通的標示非常危險。）

★ come between

It is not wise to come between other's family.（干涉人家的家務事是不智之舉。）

★ get between

Nothing can get between me and my sister.（沒有甚麼事能干擾我和姊姊間的感情。）

★ get in the way

Fury often gets in the way of judgment.（暴怒常常妨礙判斷。）

★ interfere with

I hope the habit will not interfere with my daily routine.（我希望這個習慣不會影響我日常工作。）

生活知識小補給

自信心的不足，源自於成長經驗的挫折感。在家被父母責罵，處處動輒得咎，在學校同學的嘲笑，都會是信心的重大打擊。「自信」是一個人能否成功的重要因素，雖然建立自信看似無需勞師動眾，單憑一己之力就能擁有，但對自信心不足的人來說，卻很難轉個念頭就信心滿滿。其實自信是一種技巧，能透過學習、訓練而來。你可以天天為自己信心喊話嗎？

1 Part

2 Part

3 Part

4 Part

Unit 8

北極特快車
Tight Spot.

"And time is money."
而且，時間就是金錢。

"The forsaken and the abandoned."
被人拋棄遺忘的一群。

"A tough nut to crack. We are in some serious jelly. And a jam. Tight Spot."
我們這下麻煩可大了，真棘手呀！事情大條啦，沒救囉！

🛸 動畫內容敘述

A big herd of caribous cross the railway. The conductor misunderstands that the hero boy tries to stop the train from arriving North Pole on time. The hobo estimates that there are more than a million of caribous crossing. The hero boy pulls the hobo's beard, due to the painful experience he shouts out loud. As a consequence, caribous retreat from railway and the train can finally move on. Nevertheless, the cotter pin sheared off, which causes the locomotive uncontrollably. They experience the steepest downhill grade in the world. It is like riding a roller coaster, which makes this journey a real adventure.

　　一大群的北美馴鹿跨越鐵道。列車長誤會英雄男孩故意阻止列車準時到達北極。那流動勞工估計約有一百萬隻北美馴鹿路過。英雄男孩試著拉流動勞工的鬍子，因為太痛，他大叫，卻意外地讓北美馴鹿撤離了鐵軌，而再度可以行駛。然而，開口銷的脫落，導致火車失去控制，他們駛過了一個全世界最陡峭的下坡，有如經歷雲霄飛車的冒險旅程。

（參考網站：https://en.wikipedia.org/wiki/The_Polar_Express_(film)）

 情境對話 Track 32

Allen and Jill are in an advertisement campaign. They are partners. They have a lot of dreams to achieve. The most important is that they want to win the prize-a million dollars. A few months pass by, they find out those dreams are far more too difficult than they expected.

Allen: A tough nut to crack. We are in some serious jelly. And a jam. Tight Spot. The campaign is next month. We haven't finished even half.

Jill: We made a plot which is far more than we can handle.

Allen: Sooner or later, we will be the forsaken and the abandoned.

Jill: Don't be so frustrated just now. One more month to go.

Allen: What else can we do now? My 1 million dollars...

Jill: Boohoo, stop acting like a spoiled child. We have finished half of it. Let's get moving. I still believe we have a chance of the one million dollars.

Allen: Really? How?

Jill: If we can do a little of adjustment here, that will make things easier. Then, we can definitely finish by the end of this month.

Allen: Cool, you cheer me up.

Jill: Hurry, time is money.

▶▶ 中譯

艾倫和吉兒參加廣告競賽。他們是隊友。他們有很多夢想想實現。最重要的是，他們想贏得 100 萬的獎金。幾個月過去了，他們發現夢想比他們想的還要難達到。

艾倫：我們這下麻煩可大了，真棘手呀！事情大條啦，沒救囉！下個月就要比賽了，我們一半都未完成。

吉兒：我們做了一個我們無法處理的計畫。

艾倫：很快的，我們就會變成被人拋棄遺忘的一群。

吉兒：現在別這麼沮喪。還有一個月。

艾倫：我們現在還能做甚麼？我的一百萬……

吉兒：嗚嗚，不要像個被寵壞的孩子。我們已經完成一半了，讓我們繼續做。我仍相信我們有機會得到那 100 萬。

艾倫：真的嗎？怎麼做？

吉兒：如果我們在這裡做一點調整，會把事情弄得簡單一點。我們一定可以在這個月底完成。

艾倫：太好了，你讓我精神振奮。

吉兒：快一點，時間就是金錢。

1
Part

2
Part

3
Part

4
Part

單字片語解析

forsake *v.* 遺棄

Kevin decides to forsake his smoking habit.

凱文決定戒掉他抽菸的習慣。

abandon *v.* 丟棄

Donna abandons herself to despair.

唐娜陷於絕望之中。

tough *adj.* 堅固的

This material is as tough as concrete.

這個物質有如混凝土一樣堅固。

你還可以這樣說

★ tight spot 陷入困境

也可以這麼說 be mired in difficulties

The baseball team was mired in difficulties in the final. （那棒球隊在決賽時陷入困境。）

★ get into scrapes

He often gets into scrapes while facing this kind of troubles. （他在面對這一類問題時，常常陷入困境。）

★ come to a pretty pass

Things have come to a pretty pass when kids are request-ed to put the toys in order.（當孩子被要求將玩具歸位時，事情就變得很慘。）

★ forsake 遺棄

也可以這麼說 quit

He is not happy with his working environment, so he quits his job.（他不喜歡他的工作環境，所以他辭掉他的工作。）

★ give up

Do not give up your dream too soon.（不要太快放棄你的夢想。）

生活知識小補給

　　北美馴鹿是鹿群中唯一雌雄都有角的動物。它們的角分岔相當多，最多高達 30 個分岔。母鹿的體型明顯較小，甚至有時只有公鹿的一半大小。母鹿的懷孕期約 4-6 個月，當寶寶生下來，三天即可以自由走動，而一星期後，走路速度可以和成年鹿一樣快。過去八年來，它們的數量不斷銳減，主因是惡狼會攻擊寶寶，阿拉斯加政府正研擬對策撲殺惡狼，以確保北美馴鹿不會瀕臨絕種。

1 Part

2 Part

3 Part

4 Part

Unit 9

鯊魚黑幫
I'm Dead Serious.

"Thank you for covering me."
謝謝你罩我。

"It's a fish-eat-fish world, you either take or you get taken."
這是個魚吃魚的世界，你不是砍人就是被砍。

"I'm dead serious. It takes more than muscle to run thing."
我說真的，做大事不能靠蠻力。

動畫內容敘述

Oscar brings the money, which he pawned the pearl from Angie, to the race track to meet Sykes, but becomes distracted by his dreams of being rich. On hearing that the race is rigged, he places it all on a long-shot bet by the name of "Lucky Day". Such a-million-dollar bet is noticed by a beautiful lionfish named Lola, who seduces Oscar, but Oscar is depressed when she leaves upon learning that he is merely a whale washer. Oscar brings the money to the race track to meet Sykes, who is furious that Oscar bet the money. Nonetheless, he agrees to see how the race turns out. However, Lucky Day crosses the finish line, trips and falls on the line right after they bet.

奧斯卡帶著他典當安姬的珍珠錢到賽場見史凱子，但是卻被他想致富的夢給分心了。偷聽到賽事被設計，他把錢全部賭到一隻叫「幸運日」的魚。這樣一個大賭盤，被一隻叫蘿拉的漂亮獅子魚聽到，她引誘奧斯卡。但讓奧斯卡很失望的是，她聽到他只是個洗鯨魚的清潔工時便離開了。奧斯卡帶錢去見史凱子，他很生氣他把錢賭掉。但是，他也同意看看結果如何。就在下注之後，幸運日在要到終點線前絆倒了。

（參考網站：https://en.wikipedia.org/wiki/Shark_Tale）

Part 1

Part 2

Part 3

Part 4

207

情境對話 Track 33

Zack and Victor work in a warehouse. Victor is senior. One day, a carton of goods fell on a worker, which not only hurts the worker seriously, but the goods were damaged. Boss was very angry and wanted to fire Zack. Victor stood out for him.

Zack:　Thank you for covering for me.

Victor: Our boss often tries hard to find fault with us.

Zack:　It was just an accident. I tried very hard to be careful.

Victor: I saw it. But, it's a dog-eat-dog world. You either take or you get taken.

Zack:　I did learn a lesson. Thank you so much.

Victor: Get a hold of yourself, man.

Zack:　I dodge a bullet or I have to pay through the nose.

Victor: I'm dead serious. It takes more than muscle to run things.

Zack:　Please accept my deepest gratitude.

Victor: Ok! You owe me a favor. Buy me a drink!

▶▶ 中譯

札克和維克多在倉庫工作。維克多比較資深。一天,一箱貨品掉下來壓在一個工人身上,造成工人嚴重受傷,貨品也損傷。老闆非常生氣要解雇札克。維克多挺身為他辯護。

札　　克:謝謝你罩我。

維克多:我們老闆總是努力找碴。

札　　克:那只是個意外。我已經很認真小心了。

維克多:我看到了。但是,這是個狗咬狗的世界,你不是砍人就是被砍。

札　　克:我學到了一課,真的很謝謝你。

維克多:神經繃緊一點,老兄。

札　　克:真的很驚險,否則我真要花大錢了。

維克多:我說真的,做大事不能靠蠻力。

札　　克:請接受我最深的感激。

維克多:好吧!你欠我一個人情。請我喝杯酒吧!

1
Part

2
Part

3
Part

4
Part

單字片語解析

cover *v.* 頂替

Jess always covers for her best friend to avoid her being punished.

潔絲總是罩她的好友,以免她被處罰。

either...or *ph.* 兩者任一

Either you or he should fix up the problem.

不是你就是他應該解決這個問題。

world *n.* 世界

What a fascinating world!

真是個美好的世界!

你還可以這樣說

★ dead 完全的

也可以這麼說 completely

You are completely right.(你對極了。)

★ absolutely

It absolutely has nothing to do with you.(這絕對與你無關。)

★ entirely

Her family entirely accept her new career. （她的家人完全接受她的新職業生涯。）

★ fully

I can fully understand why he did that. （我完全可以理解為何他這麼做。）

★ perfectly

It is perfectly all right to paint the wall pink. （把牆漆成粉紅色很好。）

生活知識小補給

　　賭徒的心情人人皆知，就希望受幸運之神的眷顧。但是，十賭九輸，真正能中獎的又有多少。bet 這個字相關的用法很多，老外最喜歡說 You bet!意思是 "You are right!"你對了。"The best bet is to bet on yourself." 「最好的賭就是和自己打賭。」是呀！贏過自己才是真正的贏家，沉迷於賭博，"I bet it will cost you an arm and a leg." 「我打賭一定讓你失去一隻手臂及一隻腳（所費不貲）」，您說是不是？

Unit 10

鯊魚黑幫
You Are Old School.

"Yeah, you know, one thing on top of the other. Actually, I was thinking about retiring."

是，你知道，一件事又扯出另一件事。事實上，我想退休了。

"He beat me senseless. He's a stone-cold killer, man."

他打得我不省人事。他是個冷面殺手，老兄。

"You are out. You are old school."

你完了，你過氣了。

212

動畫內容敘述

The jellyfish see Lenny and flee, leaving Oscar alone with him. Instead of attacking Oscar, Lenny frees him upsetting Frankie who becomes annoyed. Frankie is killed when an anchor falls on him. Lenny flees with grief and guilt. As no other witnesses were present and Oscar was seen near the body, everyone comes to believe that he killed Frankie, an opportunity that Oscar decides to exploit for fame. Oscar returns to the city with a new title of the Sharkslayer. Sykes becomes his manager, Lola becomes his girlfriend, and Oscar moves to the "top of the reef" to live in luxury.

　　水母看見連尼就逃跑了，單獨留下奧斯卡。連尼放了奧斯卡而沒有攻擊他，讓法蘭奇很生氣。而法蘭奇意外地被一個掉落的錨壓死。連尼悲傷地且帶有罪惡感地離開。因為沒有其他的證人，只有奧斯卡被看見他在屍體旁邊，每個人因此相信他殺了法蘭奇，也讓他有機會成為名人。奧斯卡回到城內被封為「鯊魚殺手」，史凱子變成他的經紀人，蘿拉變成他的女友，他也搬到礁岩上層住在豪華住宅內。

（參考網站：https://en.wikipedia.org/wiki/Shark_Tale）

Part 1
Part 2
Part 3
Part 4

213

 情境對話 Track 34

Ray and Andy establish the company for over half century. They are not only coworkers but also good friends. Recently, they are confronted with a dreadful competitor. Ray puts a lot of efforts on new tech products. However, the technology renews day by day. Ray thinks he is too old to catch up with.

Ray: The competitor poses a big threat to our company.

Andy: I miss the old times we had. Everything we wanted was right there in front of us the whole time.

Ray: Yeah, you know, one thing on top of the other recently. Actually, I was thinking about retiring.

Andy: You just need a little time. Things will work out.

Ray: He beat me senseless. He's a stone-cold killer, man.

Andy: They are spoiled, stupid snobs who only think about themselves.

Ray: I have to admit that if you are old school, you are out.

Andy: I guess we have to face the reality!

▶▶ 中譯

瑞和安迪建立公司超過半個世紀。他們不只是同事也是好朋友。最近，他們面對一個來勢洶洶的競爭對手。瑞盡了很大的努力在新科技產品上，然而，科技日新月異。瑞認為他太老了，追不上了。

瑞　：競爭者對我們公司造成很大的危險。

安迪：我懷念我們的舊時光。我們想要的東西，總是就在我們面前。

瑞　：是，你知道，最近一件事又扯出另一件事。事實上，我想退休了。

安迪：你只是需要一點時間，問題會解決的。

瑞　：他打得我不省人事。他是個冷面殺手，老兄。

安迪：他們是被寵壞又笨的勢利鬼，只想到他們自己。

瑞　：我必須承認，如果你過氣了，你就完了。

安迪：我猜我們必須面對現實了！

單字片語解析

retire *v.* 退休

The man retired from military 10 years ago.

那人十年前從軍隊退休。

stone-cold *adj.* 冰冷如石

The woman has a stone-cold heart.

那女人有冰冷如石的心腸。

old school *ph.* 守舊派；過時

Beeper is so called an old school gadget.

傳呼器是所謂的過時玩意兒。

你還可以這樣說

★ old school 守舊派；過時

也可以這樣說 old-line

Howard is from an old-line English family.（豪沃來自一個非常傳統的英國家庭。）

★ old guard

The man belongs to team's old guard.（那人屬於團隊的守舊派。）

★ out-of-date

This vehicle is pretty out-of-date.（這個交通工具相當過時。）

★ out of mode

Mother is still using the out of mode sewing machine.（媽媽仍在使用那個過時的縫紉機。）

★ out of fashion

The dress is out of fashion.（那件衣服過時了。）

生活知識小補給

　　住在鐵達尼號沈船內的鯊魚黑幫老大，又將我們帶到鐵達尼號，一世紀前的悲慘慘劇。這一艘船在 1912 年 4 月 14 日沈船的當夜，共有 710 人獲救，1514 人罹難。100 年過去了，正當人們對它已經淡忘時，卻又連連爆出了驚煞世人的新聞。1991 年 8 月 9 日，歐洲的一個海洋科學考察小組租用的一艘海軍搜索船正在冰島西南 387 公里處考察時，意外地發現誰也不會想到，失蹤近 80 年的「鐵達尼」號上大名鼎鼎的船長史密斯。世界掀起了「時空隧道」的研究熱潮。

1
Part

2
Part

3
Part

4
Part

Unit 11

海底總動員
Get Lost

動畫經典佳句

"It's unsafe for him to be out here unsupervised."
出去那裡沒有監管，對他不安全。

"But you have a big class and he can get lost from sight if you're not looking."
你有一個很大的班級，若你沒看著，他可能迷路。

"The first day of school, here we go! We're ready to learn to get some knowledge."
第一天上學，走吧！我們準備去學新知識。

動畫內容敘述

During a hazardous struggle with an Angler Fish in the trench, Dory sees the diving mask and reads the address located in Sydney, Australia. The pair swims on, receiving directions to Sydney from a school of Moonfish. Marlin and Dory encounter a bloom of jellyfish that nearly kills them. Marlin loses consciousness and wakes up on a sea turtle named Crush, who takes Marlin and Dory on the East Australian Current. Marlin tells the details of his long journey with a group of young turtles; his story is spread across the ocean, reaches Sydney through word of mouth. He also sees how Crush gets on well with his son Squirt. Marlin and Dory set out to find Sydney.

　　在海溝和琵琶魚奮戰時，多莉看見蛙鏡上的地址寫著澳洲雪梨。這兩隻魚繼續游，一群翻車魚告訴他們雪梨的方向。馬林和多莉碰到一堆水母，差點被電死。馬林失去意識，醒來時發現躺在一隻名叫克拉西的海龜背上，他帶著馬林和多莉到東澳洋流。馬林將他的故事告訴一群小海龜，他的故事透過口耳相傳，遠傳到整個大海，到達雪梨。他也見識了克拉西如何和他的兒子斯克爾特和睦相處。馬林和多莉出發前往雪梨。

（參考網站：http://disney.wikia.com/wiki/Finding_Nemo）

1 Part

2 Part

3 Part

4 Part

情境對話 Track 35

Erin is a very experienced teacher. He has a new class this semester. Nonetheless, a sensitive and nervous father, Victor, wants to stay in the classroom to protect his boy. Erin finds out the situation is a little difficult.

Erin: The first day of school, here we go! We're ready to learn to get some knowledge.

Victor: Sir, may I sit with my boy, Jackie.

Erin: Jackie will be fine in the classroom. Could you please just stand outside the classroom? By the way, we don't have any extra seats.

Victor: It's unsafe for him to be there unsupervised.

Erin: I will keep an eye on every student.

Victor: But you have a big class and he can get lost from sight if you're not looking.

Erin: Ok, I promise I will pay extra attention to Jackie. Would you like to do anything else before the class is over?

Victor: Ya, I have to see a dentist.

Erin: Sure, by the time you come back, Jackie will be ready to go home with you.

▶▶ 中譯

艾文是個很有經驗的老師。這學期他有一個新班級。然而,一個極度敏感及緊張的父親維克多,要留在教室保護他的兒子。艾文發現情況有點棘手。

艾　文:第一天上學,好了!我們準備學新知識。

維克多:老師,我可以和我兒子,杰克坐一起。

艾　文:杰克在教室會沒事的。可以麻煩你站到教室外面嗎?而且,我們沒多餘的座位。

維克多:那裡無人照看他,對他不安全。

艾　文:我會注意每一個學生。

維克多:你有一個很大的班級,若你沒看著,他可能迷路。

艾　文:好的,我答應一定特別注意杰克。你在課堂結束前要不要去做任何其他事?

維克多:喔,我必須去看牙醫。

艾　文:好呀,你回來的時候,杰克就可以準備和您回家了。

單字片語解析

🚩 **unsafe** *adj.* 不安全的

It is unsafe to be out at night alone for a girl.

一個女孩晚上單獨出門是很危險的。

🚩 **unsupervise** *v.* 無監督

It is dangerous for children to be unsupervised at the construction site.

孩子在工地無人監督是很危險的。

🚩 **get lost** *ph.* 迷路

The girl gets lost on the way to school.

那女孩在上學途中迷了路。

🚩 **sight** *n.* 看見

Kelly fell in love with Nick at the first sight.

凱莉在第一眼見到尼克時，就愛上他了。

🚩 **learn** *v.* 學習

We learn the importance of teamwork through the competition.

我們透過競賽，學習團隊工作的重要性。

你還可以這樣說

★ get lost 迷路

也可以這麼說 lose one's way

Ming lost his way on the mountain before calling for help.
（明在求救前在山上迷路了。）

★ go astray

The dog went astray after chasing a squirrel.（那隻狗在追一隻松鼠後迷路了。）

★ lose oneself

The old man lost himself when he was taken to a park.（當老人被帶到公園時，他就迷路了。）

生活知識小補給

活在深海中的琵琶魚是個非常有趣的生物。雌性琵琶魚有各種不同形狀及顏色，但非常醜陋。雄性琵琶魚相較之下很小，他藉由咬著母魚以附著她，接著他部分的臉部被消化，以讓他和母魚的肉身融合為一。然後他慢慢萎縮、失去消化器官、腦、心臟以及眼睛，然後最終變成一副生殖器官，需要時釋出精子。深海琵琶魚有一支由前背鰭演化而成的釣竿，釣竿上有亮亮的細菌，以創造出一個微弱的光源，因為深海裡面非常黑，需要亮光呢！

Unit 12

超人特攻隊
Set Up

"We might nab him if we set up a perimeter."
假如我們設一個範圍，我們可能抓到他。

"He put thumbtacks on my stool."
他放圖釘在我的椅子上。

"We need to find a better outlet. A more constructive outlet."
我們需要找一個好一點的發洩方式，一種更有創意的發洩方式。

動畫內容敘述

Triggered by being able to use his powers freely, Bob begins rigorous training. He claims that he is going on a business trip to his wife, Helen, takes up Mirage's offer, and travels to the island of Nomanisan in a jet with Mirage. She explains to him that the robot is called an Omnidroid, a top secret prototype battle robot, able to solve any problem it's confronted with. The only problem was its intelligence reached a point where it wondered why it was taking orders, and now it is wreaking havoc in the jungle. Mr. Incredible is then fast dropped into Nomanisan, explores around and then successfully defeat it.

被能自由使用他的超能力這樣的條件驅使著，鮑勃開始努力地訓練他自己。他跟他的妻子海倫說他要出差，帶著幻影的提議，搭著噴射機和幻影到諾曼島。她向他解釋一個叫「全能機器人」的機器人，是一個戰鬥原型機器人，可以解決任何問題。問題是他的智慧已達到他會思考為什麼他要聽從命令了，現在他正在大肆破壞一個叢林。超能先生登陸後，很快就將他打敗。

（參考網站：http://disney.wikia.com/wiki/The_Incredibles）

 Track 36

Bob is a very naughty boy. He often makes troubles at school. Mr. Rice is his homeroom teacher. He tried many ways to help and punish him, but was in vain. He feels upset. He decides to consult his coworker, Miss Richmond. She gives him a very constructive suggestion.

Mr. Rice: Bob almost drives me crazy.

Miss Richmond: What happened?

Mr. Rice: He put thumbtacks on my stool. I almost got hurt.

Miss Richmond: Is he overactive?

Mr. Rice: I'm not sure. I think he should see a doctor. He often ditches class.

Miss Richmond: You can nab him if you set up a perimeter.

Mr. Rice: He needs an outlet. I need to find a better outlet for him.

Miss Richmond: A more constructive outlet. Why not invite him to join the school baseball team?

Mr. Rice: Good idea. He enjoys playing sports. Maybe he will be a good player in the future.

Miss Richmond: Give it a shot.

▸▸ 中譯

鮑勃是個非常頑皮的男孩。他在學校常常闖禍。瑞司老師是他的班導。他試過很多方式幫他，甚至處罰他，似乎都無效。他感到很沮喪。他決定諮詢他的同事瑞奇曼老師。她給他非常有建設性的建議。

瑞司老師　：鮑勃快把我搞瘋了。

瑞奇曼老師：發生甚麼事？

瑞司老師　：他放圖釘在我的椅子上。我差點受傷。

瑞奇曼老師：他有過動嗎？

瑞司老師　：我不確定。我想他需要看醫師。他常常翹課。

瑞奇曼老師：如果你設定一個範圍，你可能抓得到他吧。

瑞司老師　：他需要一個宣洩管道。我需要替他找個好一點的發洩方式。

瑞奇曼老師：一種更有建設性的發洩方式。為什麼不邀請他加入學校棒球隊？

瑞司老師　：好主意。他很喜歡運動。可能他將來會是一個好運動員。

瑞奇曼老師：試試看吧。

1
Part

2
Part

3
Part

4
Part

單字片語解析

🚩 **nab** *v.* 抓到

Police nabbed the robber at the end.

警察最後抓到那個強盜。

🚩 **perimeter** *n.* 範圍

The teacher asked the students to play within the perimeter.

老師要求學生在範圍內玩耍。

🚩 **thumbtack** *n.* 圖釘

Please pass the box of thumbtacks to me.

請給我那一盒圖釘。

你還可以這樣說

★ set up 建立；成立

也可以這樣說 build up

We need to build up a foundation to run the charity.（我們需要成立基金會以經營慈善事業。）

★ establish

The government established regulations to rule its people.

（政府建立法規管理它的人民。）

★ take root

The action will take root and impact the market.（這個行動將成立並衝擊市場。）

★ come into existence

The principal makes the dream come into existence.（那個校長讓夢想成真。）

生活知識小補給

　　超能先生的力氣，讓人羨慕。當今金氏世界紀錄裡最強壯的男人，是世界舉重冠軍魔山(Björnsson)。擁有 206 公分的身高，體重 190 公斤的他可以說相當的猛，最具話題性的一項紀錄，就是他打破了有千年歷史的最強維京人比賽(World`s Strongest Viking)，他扛起了重 650 公斤、長 10 公尺的巨木，走了五步打破了歷史記錄。而最強壯的女生呢？沒啥肌肉的阿庫洛娃於 2000 年創下第一次金氏世界紀錄，舉起 100 公斤重，也是她的體重 40 公斤 2.5 倍重的槓鈴；2006 年更舉起 300 公斤槓鈴，超過 4 倍體重。

Part

4

生活娛樂

Unit 1

冰雪奇緣
But Only An Act of True Love Can Thaw A Frozen Heart.

動畫經典佳句

"You look beautiful-ler. I mean, not fuller. You don't look fuller, but more beautiful."
你看來比較漂亮,我說,不是較豐滿,妳不是看來較豐滿,是更漂亮。

"All my life has been a series of doors in my face."
我的人生似乎是一連串在我面前關上的門。

"But only an act of true love can thaw a frozen heart."
只有一個愛的舉動可以融化一顆冰凍的心。

動畫內容敘述

At the coronation reception, Anna's first friendly interaction with Elsa in years brings quite the delightful feeling to the princess, fluster at first but seeing Elsa so happy instead of serious and reserved boosts Anna's confidence, prompting her to continue on with the conversation. Anna comments on how well things had been going through the day, and expresses her wishes to have the things the way they are that night all the time. Elsa agrees though her smile unfortunately fades out, and she reluctantly denies Anna's wishes all at once despite failing to explain to her why all these happened.

在加冕歡迎會上，安娜在這麼多年後，第一次和艾莎這麼友善的互動，讓彼此都很開心。雖然一開始很慌張，但看到不是嚴肅和保守，卻是快樂的艾莎，讓安娜的信心高漲，促使她繼續和艾莎聊天。安娜告訴她當天事情是如何的順利，且希望當天晚上也會一直如此。艾莎也同意，雖然她的笑容很不幸地褪去，她勉強地拒絕了安娜的請求並沒解釋為什麼。

（參考網站：http://disney.wikia.com/wiki/Frozen）

1
Part

2
Part

3
Part

4
Part

Track 37

Perry and Wendy were bosom friends when they were in elementary school. Perry moved to another State after they graduated. They lost contact for many years. However, they meet again in graduate school. Life is full of miracle.

Wendy: Wow, you look beautiful-ler. I mean, not fuller. You don't look fuller, but more beautiful.

Perry: You know, I miss you so much. I always want to go back to the old times with you. At least, someone would understand me.

Wendy: What happened? See, I am here with you now. I miss you so much, too.

Perry: I was pretty upset after I moved out. It was because my parents got divorced. I felt all my life has been a series of doors in my face.

Wendy: It is not your fault. You should not blame yourself.

Perry: I am so afraid to get hurt. The only thing I did is to hide myself in the dark.

Wendy: Let me walk through this with you. I believe only an act of true love can thaw a frozen heart. I am here always with you.

Perry: Thank you, my dear.

▶▶ **中譯**

佩瑞和溫蒂是小學時的好朋友,佩瑞在畢業後搬到其他州,她們失聯了多年,但又在研究所碰到了。生命真的是一連串的驚喜。

溫蒂:哇,你看來比較漂亮,我說,不是較豐滿,妳不是看來較豐滿,是更漂亮。

佩芮:你知道,我好想你。我一直都好希望回到以前和你膩在一起的時光。至少,有人了解我。

溫蒂:發生甚麼事?你看,我現在跟你在一起了,我也好想你。

佩芮:搬家後我很難過。因為我父母離婚了。我的人生似乎是一連串在我面前關上的門。

溫蒂:那不是你的錯,你不應該自責。

佩芮:我好怕再受傷害,我只能把我自己藏在暗處。

溫蒂:讓我陪你度過。我相信只有一個愛的舉動可以融化一顆冰凍的心。我會永遠陪著你。

佩芮:謝謝你,親愛的。

 單字片語解析

beautiful *adj.*　美麗的

Christine is a beautiful girl.

克莉絲汀是個美麗的女孩。

fuller *adj.*　豐滿的

My sister looks fuller than before.

我妹妹看起來比過去豐滿。

series *n.*　連續

Police finally caught the series killer.

警察終於抓到那個連續殺人犯。

thaw *v.*　解凍；緩和

An act of smile helps to thaw out your relationship.

一個微笑的舉動能幫助緩和妳們的關係。

frozen *adj.*　冷凍的

The meat has been frozen in the freezer for 3 years.

那個肉已經在冰箱中凍了三年了。

act *n.*　行為

I don't think her act is appropriate.

我不認為她的舉止合宜。

你還可以這樣說

★ true love 真愛

你也可以這樣說 genuine love

The old lady spends all her life looking for genuine love.（那位老女士花了一輩子尋找真愛。）

★ frozen heart 淒涼

你也可以這樣說 sense of desolation

The old man walked away with a sense of desolation.（那個老人淒涼的走開了。）

★ air of sadness

The old house is full of air of sadness.（那棟老房子充滿淒涼的感覺。）

生活知識小補給

　　人生不如意十之八九，你都如何度過低潮呢？當生命陷入低潮，千萬不要自怨自艾，也不要害怕傾吐心事，更不要假裝堅強。當我在生命的低潮時，我通常會跟幾個知心好友分享，傾聽他們的意見，將朋友的意見仔細列表，分析優劣，想辦法讓自己走出困境。不過，低潮時，也常常是身體過於疲累，或精神過於緊繃導致的，這時，要學會放鬆心情，讓自己好好休息，睡個覺，走出戶外，外頭陽光正燦爛呢！

Unit 2

腦筋急轉彎
I Promise.

動畫經典佳句

"This is disgust. She basically keeps Riley from being poisoned physically and socially."

這真噁心。她基本上讓萊莉在生理上及社交上不被毒害。

"Don't worry. I am gonna make sure that tomorrow is another great day. I promise."

別擔心，我確信明天會是另一個很棒的日子。我保證。

"I don't want to get too technical, but these are called core memories."

我不想說得太技術性，但是這些叫核心記憶。

動畫內容敘述

A girl named Riley is born in Minnesota. Within her mind's Headquarters, there exist five personifications of her basic emotions: Joy, Sadness, Fear, Disgust, and Anger. The emotions influence Riley's actions via a control console. Riley's memories are stored in colored orbs, which are sent into long-term memory each night by a suction tube. Riley's most important memories, known as "core memories", are housed in a hub in Headquarters and power five "islands", each of which reflects a different aspect of Riley's personality. Joy always tries to keep Riley happy, and she and the other emotions try to prevent Sadness from using the console, not understanding her purpose.

一個叫萊莉的女孩在明尼蘇達州出生，在她的大腦總部，存在著她的五個基本情感的化身：樂樂、憂憂、驚驚、厭厭及怒怒。這些情感透過控制台影響著萊莉的行為。萊莉的記憶存在五顏六色的球，每晚由吸管傳送到長期記憶區。萊莉最重要的記憶，稱為「核心記憶」，放在總部的中心，她的五個島反映萊莉的人格特質。樂樂讓萊莉開心，她及其他情緒努力防止憂憂碰控制台，不理解她的目的為何。

(參考網站：*http://disney.wikia.com/wiki/Inside_Out*)

情境對話 Track 38

Judy and Amy are good friend. The night before their graduation, they had a long chat. They recalled many wonderful events they had gone through together...

Judy: I still remember the first day at school. I could not stop crying because I was so scared that my mum left me. You were sitting behind me and made every effort to comfort me. Miss Louise was very nice. She not only taught us but also acted as a mother to us.

Amy: Certainly, she was.

Judy: I was very sad that she left the school a few years later due to the family reasons.

Amy: Ya, I miss her so much. Even though 6 years have gone by, the memory is still so clear in my mind.

Judy: I don't want to get too technical, but I am sure those could be called our core memories. We will never forget them our whole life.

Amy: After tomorrow, we will go to different schools. I really don't wanna say goodbye to you.

Judy: Don't worry. I am gonna make sure that tomorrow is another great day. I promise.

Amy: Will we still keep in touch with each other?

Judy: Certainly.

▸▸ **中譯**

茱蒂和愛咪是好朋友。在她們畢業的前一晚，她們聊得很久。她們回憶起她們一起經歷的許多美好時刻……

茱蒂：我還記得第一天上學，我一直哭，好怕媽媽離開，你坐在我後面一直安慰我。路易斯老師真好，她不只教我們，還像媽媽一樣照顧我們。

愛咪：對呀，她是。

茱蒂：很難過她因為家庭因素，幾年後就離開學校了。

愛咪：是呀！我很想她。即使六年過去了，我的記憶還是這麼清晰。

茱蒂：我不想說得太技術性，但是這些應該叫我們的核心記憶。我們一輩子都忘不了了吧！

愛咪：明天過後，我們就要去不同的學校上學了。我真的很不想跟妳說再見。

茱蒂：別擔心，我確信明天會是另一個很棒的日子。我保證。

愛咪：我們還會保持聯絡嗎？

茱蒂：當然。

單字片語解析

disgust *v.* 噁心

I felt disgusted at the smell of fish.

聞到魚的味道我覺得很噁心。

poison *v.* 毒害

Industrial waste poisons our environment.

工業廢棄物毒害我們的環境。

core *n.* 核心

A core family consists of a father, a mother and their children.

核心家庭由一個父親，一個母親及她們的孩子組成。

prevent from *ph.* 預防

This measure cannot prevent the situation from getting worse.

這項措施無法預防情況變糟。

你還可以這樣說

★ prevent from 預防

你也可以這麼說 guard against

The police guarded against terrorists.（警察預防恐怖分子。）

★ provide against

Government tries their best to provide against the rampancy of SARS.（政府努力預防 SARS（急性呼吸道疾病）的再蔓延。）

★ promise 承諾

你也可以這麼說 give one's word

Jack gave his word to contribute his country.（傑克承諾貢獻自己的國家。）

★ agree to

He agreed to make up the loss.（他承諾彌補損失。）

生活知識小補給

　　人的情緒有相當多種，喜、怒、哀、樂、厭被視為最常見的五大情緒。腦筋急轉彎的製作，請教了相當多的心理學家及醫師，有關於人面對事情的許多情感反應。面對負面情緒，我們常常選擇壓抑，就像「憂憂」在片中常被「樂樂」阻止，這樣的行為其實是無利於人心智的健康。最後「樂樂」終於理解「憂憂」存在的價值，以及任何情緒在人的大腦總部都是相當重要的，適時的宣洩情感，才是健全心理之道。

1 Part

2 Part

3 Part

4 Part

Unit 3

怪獸大學
I Am On A Roll.

動畫經典佳句

"All right, newbies, quit goofing around."
好，新手，不要混日子了。

"I am on a roll."
我快要成功了。

"Everyone, I don't mean to get emotional, but every-thing in my life has led to the moment. Let it be just the beginning of my dream, but beginning of all of our dreams."
各位，我不想太情緒化，但我生命中的每一件事就是引導我到這個時刻。讓這個成為我夢想的開始，也是我們夢想的開始。

動畫內容敘述

Mike is so upset that his dream of being in the Scare Program has ended so soon, that he throws his book at the wall knocking down his calendar revealing a poster of the "Scare Games". That gives him the idea for getting out of his misery. Just before the end of the sign-up, Mike stands up on a car and shouts out his sign up for this new fraternity-Oozma Kappa! Everyone breaks out in a laugh as Oozma Kappa isn't really the scariest group of monsters on campus. Hardscrabble doesn't think Mike stands a chance, so he baits her into a wager. If OK wins, they must be allowed into the Scaring Program. She agrees, but also tells Mike if they lose, he will be expelled from Monsters University.

麥可很失望他夢想的驚嚇課程會這麼快結束，他把書本往牆上的日曆一丟時，日曆掉了下來，他看到一張海報寫著「驚嚇競賽」，給了他脫離悲慘命運的想法。在登記結束之前，麥可站在一台車上，大喊他登記萬事 ok 社！大家笑出來，因為這一個社團在校園內並不是最可怕的社團。郝刻薄院長不認為麥可有機會，所以他引誘她下一個賭注。如果 OK 贏了，她必須允許他們再回去上驚嚇課程。她同意，但也告訴他們，如果麥可輸了，他會被怪獸大學驅逐出去。

(參考網站：*http://disney.wikia.com/wiki/Monsters_University*)

1
Part

2
Part

3
Part

4
Part

 情境對話　Track 39

Jack is a great inventor. He is very good at making robots. Nevertheless, he needs a team to join the world robot competition. They are a group of four: Andy, Kelly and Oliver. They have a workshop to train everyone before the competition.

Jack: All right, newbies, quit goofing around.

Andy: What can we do to help?

Jack: You are all experts in your fields. I would like you to try your best in the contest.

(During the last run of competition)

Jack: Wow, a week has gone by. This is our last chance. We are on a roll.

Oliver: If we miss a shot, then we are goners. Let's get going!

Kelly: Our dream will come true soon.

(In the closing ceremony)

Jack: Everyone, I don't mean to get emotional, but everything in my life has led to this moment. Let it not be just the beginning of my dream, but the beginning of all of our dreams.

All: Bravo!

(They won the Gold Medal)

▶▶ 中譯

杰克是個很棒的發明家。他很會製作機器人。然而,他需要一個團隊參加世界機器人大賽。他們有四個人:安迪、凱莉和奧利維。在比賽前,他們有一個工作坊給每個人賽前訓練。

杰克: 好,新手,不要混日子了。

安迪: 我們需要幫什麼忙?

杰克: 你們都是你們領域的專家。我要各位在比賽中盡你所能。
（在比賽的最後一輪）

杰克: 哇,一星期過去了,這是我們的最後機會。我們快要成功了。

奧利維:如果我們錯過了,就完了。繼續努力吧!

凱莉: 我們的夢想就快成真了。
（在閉幕典禮上）

杰克: 各位,我不想太情緒化,但我生命中的每一件事就是引導我到這個時刻。讓這個成為我夢想的開始,也是我們夢想的開始。

所有人:太棒了!
（他們贏得金牌）

單字片語解析

newbie *n.* 新手

Take good care of the newbie, he needs more training.

照顧好那新手,他需要更多的訓練。

goof *v.* 犯錯

He goofed all the time.

他總是在犯錯。

roll *n.* 滾動

The share market is on the roll recently.

股市最近好運連連。

emotional *n.* 感情的

Don't be so emotional.

不要這麼情緒化。

你還可以這樣說

★ goof around 閒晃

也可以這麼說 sit around doing nothing

John sits around doing nothing during weekend.（強在週末都閒晃不做事。）

★ hang around

Stop hanging around. Do something!（不要閒晃，做一些事吧！）

★ on a roll 好運連連

也可以這麼說 lucky

He is so lucky to win the jackpot.（他好幸運贏得彩金。）

★ success

Judy has achieved a significant success in fashion industry.（茱蒂在流行事業獲得極大的成功。）

生活知識小補給

　　你有沒有曾經有一個時刻，夢想要成為電視上哪個名人？夢想要成為故事中那個偉大的英雄？逐漸成長後，你的夢想還存在嗎？如果我告訴你，你看到的名人和英雄，在他們成長過程，他們都一直往夢想前進，從不退縮，你相信嗎？你也許會問，他們完全沒有挫折嗎？沒有因為挫折而修改或甚至改變夢想嗎？是的。因為堅持，所以走到你所看見光彩的終點。海倫凱勒的故事，是否讓你我能繼續勇往直前呢？一起加油。

1 Part

2 Part

3 Part

4 Part

Unit 4

食破天驚

I Am So Looking Forward to Working With You Guys.

動畫經典佳句

"You know, I have devoted my life to inventing the future."
你知道，我貢獻我的一生發明未來。

"This is a once-in-a-lifetime opportunity."
這是千載難逢的機會。

"I am so looking forward to working with you guys."
我好期待與你們大夥兒工作。

動畫內容敍述

Chester invites Flint to work at Live Corp, where he meets Chester's assistant Barb, a talking orangoutan with human intelligence. Six months later, Flint humiliates himself during a promotion ceremony when his invention, the "Celebrationator", explodes. Meanwhile, Chester is informed that his search-parties on the island have been attacked by monstrous cheeseburgers named Cheespiders (a combination of a Cheeseburger and a Spider) which are learning how to swim. Seemingly fearing the world's inevitable doom, Chester tasks Flint to find the FLDSMDFR and destroy it once and for all. Despite Chester's demands to keep the mission classified, Flint recruits his girlfriend, meteorologist Sam Sparks; her cameraman; police officer, a monkey who communicates via a device on his chest; and "Chicken".

阿奇師邀請富林到他的公司工作。他在那裡認識了他的助理巴布，一隻有人類智慧會說話的猩猩。六個月後，他發明的「慶祝器」在晉級典禮中爆炸，使他蒙羞。同時，阿奇師被通知他的研究團隊在島嶼上被一隻正在學游泳的，像怪物的起司漢堡，叫起司蜘蛛（一種結合起司和蜘蛛的生物）所攻擊。似乎害怕世界不可預期的毀滅，阿奇師叫富林去找富拉美食複機，並將它毀掉，一勞永逸。儘管阿奇師要求該行動被指定為機密，富林仍召集了他的女友氣象學家珊、她的攝影師、警察、一隻透過它胸口設備可以溝通的猴子以及「雞」。

 Track 40

Warren is a talented engineer. He is headhunted by a company that he has long yearned for. Nevertheless, he needs to be sent to another country. His wife cannot quit her job. They discuss the future of the family.

Warren: I got an offer from X Company today.

Wife: Congratulations! It's your dream to work there.

Warren: But...I have to work in another country.

Wife: What? Can't you stay? We just bought the house and our first baby is due soon.

Warren: I know our situation now, but this is a once-in-a-lifetime opportunity.

Wife: What about me? What about us?

Warren: I know it is gonna be very hard for you.

Wife: What is your plan?

Warren: You know, I have devoted my life to inventing the future.

Wife: And...

Warren: I am so looking forward to working with them. I think I will go there and get everything settled before picking you up.

Wife: Really? Promise me, you will take us with you later.

Warren: Certainly, as long as you support me.

Wife: I will be very proud of you.

▶▶ 中譯

沃倫是個很有天分的工程師。他被一家他長久渴望的公司挖角。然而，他必須到其他國家工作。他的妻子無法放棄工作。他們討論家庭的未來。

沃倫：今天 X 公司給我一個工作。

妻子：恭喜！在那裏工作一直是你的夢想。

沃倫：但是……我必須到其他國家工作。

妻子：甚麼？你不能留下來嗎？我們才剛買房子，而且第一個孩子即將出生。

沃倫：我知道我們現在的狀況，但是這是千載難逢的機會。

妻子：那我怎麼辦？我們怎麼辦？

沃倫：我知道對你將會很辛苦。

妻子：你的計畫是什麼？

沃倫：你知道，我貢獻我的一生發明未來。

妻子：然後……

沃倫：我好期待與他們工作。我想我先過去，在接妳們過來前，把一切安頓好。

妻子：真的嗎？答應我，你會晚一點過來接我們。

沃倫：當然，只要妳支持我。

妻子：我將以你為榮。

1 Part

2 Part

3 Part

4 Part

單字片語解析

invent *v.* 發明

Hook invented a new type of microscope.

虎克發明一個新型的顯微鏡。

devote to *ph.* 貢獻於

Rick devotes himself to teaching English.

瑞克貢獻他自己於英文教學。

look forward to *ph.* 盼望

I am looking forward to your reply.

我很期盼您的回應。

你還可以這樣說

★ look forward to 盼望

也可以這樣說 expect

I expect you to visit us this year.（我期待你今年來拜訪我們。）

★ long for

Eric longs for a chance to get promoted.（艾瑞克盼望一個獲得升遷的機會。）

★ yearn for

The farmer has yearned for rain for three months.（那個農夫已經期盼下雨三個月了。）

★ wish for

The boy wishes for Christmas gifts from Santa Claus.（那男孩盼望聖誕老公公送給他聖誕禮物。）

★ hope for

The villagers hope for a thriving year.（鄉民盼望一個繁盛的一年。）

生活知識小補給

臉書，人人皆知的公司，一流頂尖大學的學生擠破頭都想拿到進去實習的機會。工程部經理的年薪高達 38 萬美元，一般的軟件工程師也有 12 萬美元的年薪，就連實習生的月薪亦可達 6,058 美元。聽起來真是很棒的一家公司。但是，規定一年有 6 週隨時待命，週末也無法離開。每天都有超過 1,600 封內部溝通的電子郵件要回，而且，因為是在臉書工作，所以大部份時間都掛在臉書上。看來要在一流公司上班，也不是一件容易的事呢！

動畫經典佳句

"Hey, you gave it your best shot, right? What more can you do?"

嘿，這是你最好的嘗試，對嗎？你可以再多做甚麼？

"I say I would keep an eye on you."

我說我會監視你。

"I won't let you down."

我不會讓你失望。

動畫內容敘述

Over the visits, the Once-ler recounts the story of how he met the Lorax, a grumpy yet charming creature who serves as guardian of the land he arrived in and actively resists his logging until the Once-ler agrees to desist. When the young businessman introduces a revolutionary invention from the native Truffula Tree's tufts, the thneed, it eventually becomes a major success and the Once-ler's family is brought in to participate in the business. Keeping his promise at first, Once-ler continues thneed production by harvesting the tufts themselves in a sustainable manner. Unfortunately, his greedy and lazy relatives convinced him to resume logging as a more efficient gathering method, and the destruction of the forest spirals into a mass overproduction.

在幾次拜會，萬事樂說他如何遇到羅雷司。一個性情乖戾但迷人的生物，他守護他所在的土地，並抵抗萬事樂直到他同意停止砍伐。當這個年輕人引進了改革式的，從松露樹的毛叢發明的「絲尼」後，獲得了輝煌的成功，並發展成萬事樂家族事業。為了守住承諾，萬事樂持續收成毛叢生產絲尼。很不幸地，他那些貪心、懶惰的親戚說服他，要繼續砍伐樹木才會更有效率的收成。森林的破壞也造成了過度的生產。

（參考網站：https://en.wikipedia.org/wiki/The_Lorax）

1
Part

2
Part

3
Part

4
Part

 情境對話 Track 41

David is a potential basketball player. Yet, he does not have confidence on himself. His coach, Tommy, believes he will be a super star one day. He tries very hard to encourage him and makes him believe that he can challenge his ultimate.

Tommy: Are you ready for the tournament next week?

David: I am not sure. Unfortunately, I just recovered from a terrible cold.

Tommy: I know it's hard. You should not only pay attention to your health but also concentrate on practicing.

David: I am afraid I cannot meet your expectations.

Tommy: Don't worry about my expectations. Let's do some practices.

(After few shots, he did not miss any.)

Tommy: Hey, you gave it your best shot, right? What more can you do?

David: I hope I will not divert my focus in the game.

Tommy: Exactly, I will keep an eye on you. Here is the chicken soup my wife made for you. You should get more rest this week.

David: Thank you. I won't let you down.

▶▶ 中譯

大衛是個很有天賦的球員。然而，他對他自己沒有信心。他的教練，湯米，相信他有一天將會成為超級明星。他很努力地鼓勵他，並讓他相信他可以挑戰他的極限。

湯米：你準備好下星期的比賽了嗎？

大衛：我不確定。很不幸地，我感冒才剛好。

湯米：我知道很辛苦。你不只要注意身體，還要專心練習。

大衛：我擔心我無法符合您的期待。

湯米：別擔心我的期待，讓我們做一些練習。

　　　（投幾次籃，他球球進籃。）

湯米：嘿，這是你最好的嘗試，對嗎？你可以再多做甚麼？

大衛：我希望我在比賽中不要分心。

湯米：對，我會看著你。這是我太太為你熬的雞湯。這星期你該多休息。

大衛：謝謝您，我不會讓您失望的。

單字片語解析

🏴 **shot** *n.* 嘗試

Tony made a good shot at the baseball game.

東尼在那棒球賽做了很好的嘗試。

🏴 **down** *adj.* 情緒低落的

I felt down this morning.

我今天早上感到情緒低落。

🏴 **keep an eye on sb.** *ph.* 注意某人

Teachers always keep an eye on their students.

老師總是注意著他們的學生。

🏴 **let sb. down** *ph.* 讓某人失望

I promise not to let my mother down.

我承諾不會讓我媽失望。

你還可以這樣說

★ keep an eye on＋人 注意某人

也可以這麼說 watch

I will watch you.（我會注意你。）

★ pay attention to

Could you pay attention to my boy while I am away?（你可以在我不在時注意一下我兒子嗎？）

★ let 人 down 失望

也可以這麼說 lose hope

We will not lose hope on him.（我們不會對他失去希望。）

★ disappoint

Eric is disappointed that he fails in the test.（艾瑞克對他考試失敗很失望。）

生活知識小補給

　　大家應該還記得，在 2016 年的一月，台灣很多城市都下了類似雪的霰，令人興奮。溫度降到零度以下，是空前的氣象紀錄。氣象局努力告訴大家，因為「北極震盪」的關係，溫暖的台灣下起厚厚的雪。北極震盪，冷空氣的外擴，造成北極以外地區變得極度寒冷，而北極暖化融冰現象，逐漸嚴重，不只北極熊瀕臨絕跡，低窪地區也即將面臨滅頂的慘狀。大家在興奮之餘，也許想想，許多城市將變成未來的亞特蘭提斯，令人不寒而慄呀！

Unit 6

鯊魚黑幫
You Are Unbelievable.

動畫經典佳句

"Truer words have never been spoken. Is that it? We done?"

真話都不會講出來。真是這樣嗎？我們完了嗎？

"You are unbelievable. You're in trouble up to your gills and still you're askin' for more."

你真的令人難以置信，火燒到屁股了還到處捅婁子。

"I never told you two this, but you are the best henchman a guy ever had."

我從來沒告訴你們兩個，但是你們真是我最好的手下。

動畫內容敘述

When Oscar runs into Lenny, Lenny forces Oscar to let him stay with him since he is aware of Oscar's lie. Soon, Angie finds out about the lie and threatens to tell everyone. Oscar and Lenny convince her to keep quiet, though she is heartbroken by Oscar's dishonesty. Oscar's situation is not helped by Lola, who tells him that her interest in him only extends as far as he remains famous. Oscar and Lenny stage an event in which Lenny pretends to terrorize the town and Oscar must defeat him throwing him into the depths of the ocean. Though this further steadies Oscar as the Sharkslayer, it greatly angers Don Lino.

當奧斯卡撞見連尼，連尼強迫他讓他留下，因為連尼知道奧斯卡在說謊。很快的，安姬發現謊言並威脅要告訴大家。他們說服安姬保持安靜，雖然她因奧斯卡的不誠實心碎了。蘿拉也不幫忙，她告訴奧斯卡，她只對他成為名人有興趣。所以連尼和奧斯卡計畫一場戲，連尼假裝威脅城市，奧斯卡打敗他，把他丟到深海。雖然這樣的戲更鞏固了鯊魚殺手名號，卻也惹得湯大尾更不高興。

（參考網站：https://en.wikipedia.org/wiki/Shark_Tale）

1
Part

2
Part

3
Part

4
Part

 情境對話 Track 42

Brant is a not-so-smart Italian politician. Elliott works for him for more than 10 years. Brant sometimes needs to flatter the Mafia, Elliott can always nail it. This time, the Mafia requests more, Brant is too scare to say no to them.

Brant: Truer words have never been spoken. Is that it? We done?

Elliott: What are you gonna do with them?

Brant: I really have no idea. I shouldn't have been so close to them. But I need votes.

Elliott: You are unbelievable. You're in trouble up to your gills and still you're askin' for more.

Brant: Ok, the motion they ask is illegal. They said if I do not support them, they will let me learn the consequence.

Elliott: What if you deal with the matter under the table with other politicians?

Brant: How?

Elliott: Ask them to veto the motion.

Brant: How could I convince the Mafia?

Elliott: Tell them, the motion was lost by a majority.

Brant: Brilliant. Then, it will not be my fault. I never told you this, but you are the best henchman a guy ever had.

▶▶ **中譯**

布蘭特是個不太聰明的義大利政治人物。艾略特為他工作超過十年。布蘭特有時需要巴結黑手黨,艾略特總是能夠搞定。這一次,黑手黨要求更多,布蘭特因太害怕而不敢對他們說不。

布蘭特:真話都不會講出來。真是這樣嗎?我們完了嗎?

艾略特:你要怎麼處理?

布蘭特:我真的不知道。我不應該跟他們靠太近,但我需要選票呀!

艾略特:你真的令人難以置信,火燒到屁股了還到處捅簍子。

布蘭特:好吧,他們要求的動議是非法的。他們說我若不支持他們,他
　　　　們要讓我自負後果。

艾略特:如果你在檯面下跟其他政治人物處理這件事呢?

布蘭特:怎麼做?

艾略特:請他們否決動議。

布蘭特:那我怎麼說服黑手黨?

艾略特:告訴他們,動議被多數否決了。

布蘭特:聰明,那就不會是我的錯了。我從來沒告訴你,但是你真是我
　　　　最好的手下。

單字片語解析

▶ **gill** *n.* 魚鰓

Gills are the fish organ that helps breathing.

鰓是魚幫助呼吸的器官。

▶ **henchman** *n.* 忠實的追隨者（為有權勢人士從事不良、非法事務）

Henry is a henchman for the politician.

亨利是那個政治人物的忠實的追隨者。

▶ **guy** *n.* 傢伙

What you guys are doing?

你們這些傢伙在做甚麼？

你還可以這樣說

★ unbelievable 令人難以置信的

也可以這樣說 hard to believe

It is hard to believe that Jim passed the exam.（很難令人相信吉姆通過考試。）

★ beyond belief

The rescue team beyond belief saved all the victims.（那救援隊令人難以置信的救了所有的受難者。）

★ incredible

The story he told was incredible.（他説的那個故事令人難以置信。）

★ ask for 要求

也可以這樣説 request

The teacher requests all the students to hand in homework by next week.（那老師要求所有學生在下星期前交出作業。）

★ demand

The mother demands her children to put their toys in order.（媽媽要求她的孩子將玩具整理好。）

生活知識小補給

　　鯊魚究竟有多少牙齒？鯊魚的牙齒並不是直接固定在顎上，而是嵌在牙齦中，數量也不一定，約有 5-6 排，除最外排起到真正牙齒的功用，其餘都是「仰臥」備用。它們的牙齒在一生中會不斷的被更新替換，有些鯊魚在一生中甚至會替換掉 3 萬顆以上的牙齒。替換用的牙齒原本長在上下顎內的溝槽中，接著慢慢像輸送帶一樣的往前移動替補。替換的頻率從 10 天左右到數個月都有可能。

Unit 7

北極特快車
In Case

👑 動畫經典佳句

"In case you didn't know, that card is for emergency purposes only."

怕你不知道，那張卡是緊急時用的。

"It's a violation of safety regulation for a kid to cross moving cars without a grown-up."

對一個孩子走過移動車廂，沒有大人帶，是違反安全規定。

"This is an official, authentic, genuine ticket to ride."

這是一個正式的火車票，如假包換喔。

動畫內容敘述

The boy meets other children, including a girl and a know-it-all kid. Billy initially declines to board but changes his mind. The hero boy applies the emergency brakes to stop the train and to pick Billy up. The conductor summons a waiter team to serve the children hot chocolate. The hero girl stows away one cup under her seat to give to Billy, who is alone in the observation car. The girl and conductor deliver the hot chocolate cup to Billy until the hero boy discovers the girl's ticket is unpunched. He loses it before he can return it. After the ticket is abused by the wind and animals, it slips back in the train.

那男孩在火車上遇到許多其他孩子，包括一個女孩及萬事通。比利本來不想上車的，後來改變心意，英雄男孩就拉緊急剎車，讓比利上車。列車長叫一群服務人員給孩子們熱巧克力喝。那個英雄女孩放了一杯在座位下，為了留給比利喝，因為他一個人留在觀察室。女孩和列車長將熱巧克力送過去給比利時，英雄男孩發現女孩沒有打洞的車票留在座位上。他在還車票過程中，竟遺失車票。而車票在風中飄雪地飛，卻又戲劇性的回到車廂中。

（參考網站：*https://en.wikipedia.org/wiki/The_Polar_Express_(film)*）

 情境對話 Track 43

Terry and two of his classmates won the gold medal in the Science Fair Competition. They win themselves a trip to Japan and experience the Maglev (magnetic levitation vehicle). Their teacher gave them a card and a ticket each before their departure. They are very excited to experience the fastest train in the world.

Conductor: Welcome aboard. Ticket, please.

Terry: Thank you. I don't know which one I should use.

Conductor: The ticket on your right hand.

Terry: OK. I cannot read Japanese.

Conductor: This is an official, authentic, genuine ticket to ride.

Terry: What about this card?

Conductor: That card is for emergency purposes only.

Terry: OK. How fast will we go?

Conductor: We will go at about 600 km per hour.

Terry: Wow, that's pretty awesome.

Conductor: I would like to remind you that it's a violation of safety regulations for a kid to cross moving cars without a grown-up.

Terry: I was just wondering if I could stand steadily in the car.

Conductor: You had better remain seated and fasten your seat belt.

Terry: Certainly, sir. I couldn't wait to ride on.
Conductor: Enjoy the trip.

▶▶ 中譯

泰瑞和他的兩個同學在科展贏得冠軍。他們贏得到日本的旅遊,並可以體驗磁浮列車。老師在他們出發前給每人一張票及一張卡。他們對能體驗世界最快的火車都感到非常興奮。

列車長:歡迎上車,請拿出車票。

泰　瑞:謝謝,我不知道我應該用哪一張。

列車長:在你右手的票。

泰　瑞:好的,我不懂日文。

列車長:這是一個正式的火車票,如假包換喔。

泰　瑞:那這個卡是甚麼?

列車長:那張卡是緊急時用的。

泰　瑞:好的。我們會開多快?

列車長:我們會開大約每小時 600 公里。

泰　瑞:哇,超棒的。

列車長:我要提醒你,小孩走過移動車廂,沒有大人帶,是違反安全規定。

泰　瑞:我還在想我在車廂內是否能站穩呢!

列車長:你最好坐著並繫好你的安全帶。

泰　瑞:好的,先生。我等不及要上車了。

列車長:祝您旅途愉快。

單字片語解析

emergency *n.* 緊急情況

In case of emergency, please call 119.

緊急情況請打 119。

violation *n.* 違犯

It is a violation of traffic regulation, if a driver drives after drinking alcohol.

如果一個司機在喝酒後駕車，就是違反交通規則。

regulation *n.* 法規

The government set up a regulation to avoid smuggling.

政府訂定法規避免走私。

你還可以這樣說

★ in case 假如

也可以這樣說 if

If you have time, please come and visit us.（假如你有時間，請來拜訪我們。）

★ provided that

I will accept the offer provided that the company allows me to work at home.（我會接受這個工作，若公司允許我在家工作。）

★ supposing

Wear the sunscreen lotion supposing you don't want to get sun burn.（如果你不想被曬傷，擦防曬油。）

★ grown-up 成年人

也可以這樣說 adult

This animation is for adult.（這一個動畫電影是為大人設計的。）

★ a full-grown man

Being a full-grown man, you need to learn the consequence.（作為一個成人，你要學會承受後果。）

生活知識小補給

　　目前世界上最快的傳統軌道火車是法國的 TGV，它的最高時速在 2007 年打破紀錄，以 574.8 公里時速行駛。筆者曾坐在 TGV 上，快速的火車，行駛時，耳壓的平衡成為一項挑戰。而非傳統軌道的，則是日本 JR 的磁浮列車，時速可以高達 603 公里／小時，使用磁浮軌道。美國人設計的無人火箭滑車（rocket sleds）靠軌道的協助，可達到時速 10,400 公里，這樣的速度，不知人類坐在上頭是否能承受。

Unit 8

北極特快車
Seeing Is Believing.

動畫經典佳句

"But sometimes seeing is believing. And sometimes the most real thing in the world are the things we can't see."

但，有時候眼見為憑。有時候世界上最真實的事就是我們看不見的東西。

"But I know it was just an optical illusion."

但是我知道它只是個幻覺。

"Cutting it kind of close, aren't we?"

來得早不如來得巧，是嗎？（真是千鈞一髮呀！）

動畫內容敘述

Upon arrival, the hero boy and girl see Billy depressed and alone in the observation car. They want to encourage Billy to go, but the carriage is uncoupled after the hero boy accidentally stepped on the latch, rolls downhill backwards, and stops on a turntable. The three kids explore the city's industrial area until falling on a pile of presents, which are transported in a giant bag. The giant bag is placed on Santa's sleigh, and elves remove the kids. As the reindeer are prepared, Santa arrives. One bell breaks loose from a harness, and the hero boy retrieves it. He first hears nothing, but when he believes, he hears a sound. Santa entrusts the boy the bell as "The first gift of Christmas".

到達目的地之後，英雄男孩和女孩看到比利沮喪單獨的留在觀察車廂內。他們要鼓勵比利一起去，但車廂因為英雄男孩意外踩到一個閂把，脫鈎，滑到軌道另一頭的轉車台那。三個孩子在生產區探險，直到跌落至一個巨大的袋子中的一堆禮物裡。大袋子放在聖誕老人的雪橇中，然後精靈把孩子們帶出來。當馴鹿準備好，聖誕老人來了，一個鈴鐺從馬彎頭上滑落，英雄男孩將它放回。剛開時他聽不見任何音樂，但他相信後，他聽見美麗的音樂。聖誕老人將鈴鐺送給男孩，並稱為「聖誕節第一個禮物」。

（參考網站：https://en.wikipedia.org/wiki/The_Polar_Express_(film)）

1 Part

2 Part

3 Part

4 Part

情境對話 Track 44

Henry had a fight with his parents. He left home and idled away his time on the streets for few weeks. He does not have a job and runs out the pocket money. On the New Year Eve, he sits on a bench with a wise man and experiences the countdown. He shares his story with the wise man.

Wise Man: What is your plan next? You should have some new year's resolutions.

Henry: I don't know. No one would hire me since I only graduated from high school.

Wise Man: Why not go back to school?

Henry: I don't have money.

Wise Man: Young man, I would suggest you go home and say sorry to your parents.

Henry: How should I put this?

Wise Man: Sometimes the most real thing in the world are the things we can't see.

(The firework)

Henry: How amazing, fireworks! Beautiful!

Wise Man: I know, but it is just an optical illusion. The most beautiful thing is family.

(Suddenly, Henry's mother stands behind him.)

Henry: Mum?

Wise Man: Cutting it kind of close, aren't we? There is no place like home.

Henry: Thank you.

▸▸ 中譯

亨利跟父母吵架,他離家並在街頭閒晃幾星期。他沒有工作而且口袋的錢用光了。在除夕夜,他在公園的椅子上跟一位智者坐一起,體驗跨年倒數。他跟智者分享他的故事。

智者:你下一步要怎麼做?你應該有一些新年新希望吧!

亨利:我不知道。我只有高中畢業,沒有人要雇用我。

智者:為何不回學校去?

亨利:我沒有錢。

智者:年輕人,我建議你回家跟父母道歉。

亨利:我該怎麼說呢?

智者:有時候世界上最真實的事就是我們看不見的東西。

　　　(煙火)

亨利:好棒呀,煙火!真漂亮!

智者:我知道,但這些都只是幻象。家才是最美的東西。

　　　(突然間,亨利的媽媽站在他後面。)

亨利:媽?

智者:來得早不如來得巧,是嗎?沒有一個地方比家裡好。

亨利:謝謝您。

單字片語解析

optical　*adj.*　眼睛的；光學的

The optical device is to measure eyesight.

這個光學儀器是用來測量視力的。

illusion　*n.*　幻覺

Mirage is only an illusion.

海市蜃樓只是一種幻覺。

cut it close　*ph.*　千鈞一髮

You are cutting it too close; you just stop right in front of the cliff.

你剛好停在懸崖前，真是千鈞一髮呀！

你還可以這樣說

★ Seeing is believing. 眼見為憑

也可以這麼說 To see is to believe.

To see is to believe. I will not follow the crowd.（眼見為憑，我不會跟著一窩蜂行動。）

★ optical illusion 錯覺

也可以這麼說 delusion

Ken suffers from delusion.（肯深受幻覺之苦。）

★ hallucination

The ghost he saw was only hallucination. （他看到的鬼只是幻覺而已。）

★ mistaken impression

One suffering from mental illness often has a mistaken impression on something or someone. （精神病患常對某人或某事有幻覺。）

生活知識小補給

　　你相信眼見為憑嗎？藝術家運用了許多錯覺藝術，欺騙你的大腦，利用色彩及圖像的誤導，讓你的大腦產生幻覺。其實這跟我們眼睛構造有很大的關係。成人的視網膜約 72%在 22釐米的球體。在視網膜中間是個光學圓盤，也稱為「盲點」，因為它缺乏視覺感受器，而每一個人盲點位置也不同，這也就是幻覺產生的原因。所以這也可以解釋，為何有一些人非常固執於成見，因為他們深信「眼見為憑」囉！

1 Part

2 Part

3 Part

4 Part

Unit 9

海底總動員
Slow Down

動畫經典佳句

"See, I suffer from short-term memory loss. It runs in my family."
看，我有短暫記憶喪失的問題，這是家族遺傳。

"Slow down, little fella. There's nothing to worry about."
慢一點，小東西，沒甚麼好擔憂的。

"When life gets you down know what you got to do?"
當生活讓你沮喪，你知道該做甚麼嗎？

動畫內容敘述

Nemo is placed in a fish tank in the office of a dentist named Phillip Sherman on Sydney Harbour. He meets aquarium fish called the Tank Gang, led by a Moorish Idol named Gill, who has a broken fin. The fish learn that Nemo is to be given to Sherman's niece, Darla, who killed a fish by constantly shaking its bag. Gill then reveals his plan to escape, jamming the tank's filter, forcing the dentist to remove the fish to clean it. The fish would be placed in plastic bags, and then they would roll out the window and into the harbor. After an attempt at the escape goes wrong, a brown pelican, Nigel, brings news of Marlin's adventure.

尼莫被帶回到雪梨港一個叫皮雪曼的牙醫師的牙醫診所。他遇見一隻水族缸的魚唐剛，由一隻有壞掉的鰭叫奇哥的鐮魚所領導。這些魚得知尼莫將要被送給皮雪曼那個曾一直猛搖塑膠袋導致魚死亡的姪女，達拉。奇哥透露他的逃脫計畫，把魚缸的過濾器堵住，強迫牙醫將他們拿出來清洗魚缸。魚將被放在塑膠袋內，他們就會滾動塑膠袋，滾進漁港。計畫失敗時，一隻叫耐吉的鵜鶘帶來馬林的冒險故事。

（參考網站：http://disney.wikia.com/wiki/Finding_Nemo）

情境對話 🎧 Track 45

Maggie is a social worker. One day, she notices a teenage girl wandering around. It looks like she is lost. Maggie thinks it is not safe for a little girl hanging out alone. She approaches her and finds out her name is Rose.

Maggie: Rose, it looks like you are lost.

Rose:　　I couldn't find my way home.

Maggie: What happened? Can I help?

Rose:　　I suffer from short-term memory loss. It runs in my family.

Maggie: What else can you remember?

Rose:　　I cannot remember why I am here. I am so hungry and cold. Boohoo...

Maggie: Slow down, little one. There's nothing to worry about.

Rose:　　I want my mother.

Maggie: Let me get something for you to eat first. Then, I will help you to find your mother.

Rose:　　Thank you. I have a piece of paper in my pocket.

Maggie: Let me see.

　　　　(The paper clearly states the girl's details and address)

Maggie: When life gets you down know what you got to do?

Rose:　　Um...

Maggie: Never lose hope. God will send you an angel. OK?

▶▶ **中譯**

美姬是個社工。一天，她注意到一個十多歲的女孩在閒晃，看起來她好像迷路了。美姬認為一個女孩單獨在外閒逛不安全。她走向她，發現她叫羅絲。

美姬：羅絲，看起來你好像迷路了。

羅絲：我找不到路回家。

美姬：發生甚麼事？我可以幫你嗎？

羅絲：我有短暫記憶喪失的問題，這是家族遺傳。

美姬：你還記得甚麼？

羅絲：我記不得為什麼我在這裡。我好餓好冷。嗚嗚嗚嗚嗚……

美姬：慢一點，小東西，沒甚麼好擔憂的。

羅絲：我要找媽媽。

美姬：讓我先弄東西給你吃。然後，我幫你找媽媽。

羅絲：謝謝你。我口袋有一張紙。

美姬：讓我看。

（那張紙清楚寫著女孩的資料及她的地址）

美姬：當生活讓你沮喪，你知道該做甚麼嗎？

羅絲：嗯……

美姬：永遠別失去希望，上帝會為你帶來天使。好嗎？

單字片語解析

🏴 **suffer** *v.* 遭受

That old lady has suffered from osteoporosis for 10 years.

那老女士已遭受 10 年的骨質疏鬆症。

🏴 **short-term** *adj.* 短期的

This is a short-term sewing class.

這是一個短期縫紉課程。

🏴 **fella** *n.* 夥伴

They were fellas on the school team.

他們在學校團隊是夥伴。

你還可以這樣說

★ down 情緒低落；失望

也可以這麼說 lose hope

We shouldn't lose our hope on our lives.（我們不應對我們的生活失望。）

★ get the cheese

The carpenter got the cheese at the end.（那木匠最後失望了。）

★ worry 擔心；擔憂

也可以這麼說 be anxious

The doctor is anxious to look for the cure of the disease.（醫師焦慮地尋找疾病的治療方法。）

★ feel concerned about

John feels concerned about his missing dog.（約翰憂慮他走失的狗。）

★ tremble for

People tremble for the deterioration of weather.（人們擔心天氣的惡化。）

生活知識小補給

　　鵜鶘，讓大家印象深刻的就是卡通故事的送子鳥。牠們一袋袋的帶著嬰兒到人們家中的形象，讓這樣的鳥類深植人心。現實生活中，身長可達 180 公分的鵜鶘，是個巨型鳥類，它的巨大囊袋可以裝下 9 公升的水。鵜鶘對配偶可是非常忠心耿耿，一旦配對，終生不換。牠們一窩可以生下 1-4 隻小雛鳥，雛鳥的食物，則是多由父母消化過的食物，吐出來餵哺下一代。成鳥則要到 3-4 歲才會完全成熟。比起鳥類動物，成長速度相當的慢呢！

Unit 10

海底總動員
It's A Foolproof.

♛ 動畫經典佳句

"I'm thinking, tonight, we give the kid a proper reception."

我在想，今晚，我們給那孩子一個歡迎會。

"You really nailed him. It's a foolproof."

你們真的搞定他。萬無一失。

"I think you are nuts."

我想你是個瘋子。

動畫內容敘述

Marlin sees Nemo and believes he is dead before Nigel is thrown out. Marlin leaves Dory and begins to swim home in despair. Gill then helps Nemo escape into a drain that leads to the ocean. Dory loses her memory and becomes confused, and meets Nemo, who reached the ocean. Eventually, Dory's memory returns after she reads the word "Sydney" on a drainpipe. She directs Nemo to Marlin and they reunite, but then Dory is caught in a fishing net with a school of Grouper. Nemo enters the net and orders the group to swim downward to break the net, enabling them to escape. After returning home, Nemo leaves for school, and Marlin, no longer over-protective, proudly watches Nemo swim away with Dory at his side.

馬林在耐吉被丟出去前看到尼莫，以為他死了。馬林傷心地離開多莉，開始游回家。奇哥幫助尼莫跳到一個通道大海的下水道孔。多莉失去記憶，變得很困惑，她碰到回到大海的尼莫，當她看到下水道管上「雪梨」的兩個字，又讓她記起來了。她帶尼莫去找馬林，讓他們重逢，但多莉卻跟一群魚被魚網撈住。尼莫進入漁網，命令所有的魚往下游將魚網弄破，逃出網。回到家後，不再過度保護的馬林，很驕傲地看著尼莫和多莉一起上學。

（參考網站：http://disney.wikia.com/wiki/Finding_Nemo）

1 Part
2 Part
3 Part
4 Part

 情境對話 Track 46

Angela and Bernice are roommates. They just informed by their landlord that they are going to have a new roommate, Dale. They want to give him a big surprise when he arrives.

Angela: Gee, it's a boy.

Bernice: Well, I hope the room is not gonna be dirty soon.

Angela: I am worried about the toilet.

Bernice: Hope he is a boy with good manners.

Angela: Should we set up a list of room rules?

Bernice: I'm afraid he will not follow them.

Angela: I'm thinking, tonight, we give the kid a proper reception.

Bernice: Why not? How are we gonna do it?

Angela: We are gonna mess up the whole apartment.

Bernice: I think you are nuts. Why do you do so?

Angela: It's foolproof. If we keep asking him to make the room clean, it will be a tedious thing.

Bernice: Wow, negative impact. Bravo! You can really nail him.

▶▶ 中譯

安琪拉和伯妮絲是室友。房東剛通知她們將有一位新室友，戴爾。她們想給他一個大驚喜。

安琪拉：天啊，是個男孩。

伯妮絲：唉，我希望房間不會很快變髒。

安琪拉：我擔心廁所呢！

伯妮絲：真希望他是個有禮貌的男孩。

安琪拉：我們要訂個房規嗎？

伯妮絲：我很擔心他根本不會照做。

安琪拉：我在想，今晚，我們給那孩子一個歡迎會。

伯妮絲：好呀！我們要怎麼做？

安琪拉：我們把整間公寓弄得很髒。

伯妮絲：我想你是個瘋子。你幹嘛這麼做？

安琪拉：這一定是萬無一失。你如果一直叫他把房間清乾淨會很煩。

伯妮絲：哇，負面衝擊。太棒了！你可以搞定他。

單字片語解析

foolproof *adj.* 笨人也能懂的；超簡單的

The operation of this machine is foolproof.

這個機器的操作超簡單。

nuts *n.* 瘋子

Are you nuts?

你是瘋子？

nail *v.* 搞定

The know-it-all announces he can nail everything.

那個萬事通先生宣稱他可以搞定所有事。

你還可以這樣說

★ It's a foolproof. 萬無一失。

也可以這麼說 no danger of anything going wrong

This business is no danger of anything going wrong.（這件生意萬無一失。）

★ no risk at all

The stock broker guarantees this purchase will be no risk at all.（那股票經紀人保證這個採購萬無一失。）

★ perfectly safe

With the prevention measures, the factory will be perfectly safe.（有這個預防措施，工廠將絕對安全。）

★ surefire

The action will be surefire.（這個行動一定成功。）

★ certain to succeed

The performance is certain to succeed since we have done so many practices.（我們已經做了這麼多練習，表演一定成功。）

生活知識小補給

雪梨歌劇院(Sydney Opera House)，這個代表 20 世紀的偉大建築，是由瑞典的建築師 Jorn Utzon 所設計。許多人推測這個特有的形狀，其構想來自於貝殼，也有人臆測，這應該是風帆的形狀，甚至猜想是海浪拍打岸上給他的巧思。經過幾十年後，在一次的專訪，Jorn 終於說出這一個構想的秘密，原來他是在想設計圖時，妻子為他端上一盤切好的柳橙。這一片片的柳橙，堆疊出來的美麗建築設計圖，讓他在眾多名建築師設計圖中脫穎而出。

Unit 11

超人特攻隊
Bring Sb. Lower

動畫經典佳句

"Disregarding life is not strength and value life is not weakness."

忽視生命不是勇敢，珍惜生命不是弱點。

"How can you possibly bring me lower? What more can you take away from me?"

你怎麼可以再打擊我？你還可以從我這拿去甚麼？

"Let go, you lousy, lying, unfaithful creep!"

滾，你這厭煩的、說謊的不忠實的卑鄙小人！

動畫內容敘述

Helen borrows a private jet from an old friend and travels to the island, but finds Violet and Dash have stowed away wearing their own suits. Syndrome picks up Helen's radio transmissions and gives an order to terminate them by hitting the plane with missiles. Elastigirl uses her superpower to save her children from the exploding jet, and they safely make it ashore. Helen, Violet and Dash take shelter during that night in a cave and Elastigirl runs off to Syndrome's lair. Helen gives Violet and Dash masks to protect their identity and makes them promise to use their powers if threatened before she departs.

　　海倫向一個老朋友借一架噴射機到小島上，發現小倩和小飛穿著他們的超人衣服藏在飛機內。辛拉登追蹤到海倫，並命令用一枚飛彈將他們打下來。彈力女超人用她的超能力救孩子們逃出爆炸的飛機，然後安全的上岸。那天晚上海倫、小倩和小飛躲在一個山洞裡，然後海倫直搗辛拉登基地。在海倫離開前，她給小倩和小飛一個面具以保護他們的身分曝光，並要他們承諾遇到威脅要用超能力保護自己。

　　(參考網站：http://disney.wikia.com/wiki/The_Incredibles)

 情境對話 Track 47

Bruce is a bully in the neighborhood. Morgan is a gentle, careful and considerate good boy. One afternoon, Morgan sees Bruce and his fellows kick a hobo on the street. Morgan is afraid that the hobo might get killed. He decides to stand out for the hobo to beg their pardon.

Morgan: Could you show a little mercy? He is innocent.

Bruce:　No intervention ! Darn you! You should never take sides against me.

Morgan: Man, I'm not explaining myself to you, but this is not right.

Bruce:　You are such a loser. He is useless. You cannot protect him.

Morgan: Disregarding life is not strength and value life is not weakness.

Bruce:　I know your moves. Stupid, little stick figure...

Morgan: How can you possibly bring me lower?

Bruce:　You sly dog! You got me monologuing.

Morgan: Let go, you lousy, lying, unfaithful creep!

▸▸ **中譯**

布魯斯是鄰里的惡霸。摩根是個溫和、小心和體貼的好男孩。一天下午，摩根看到布魯斯和他的同夥在街上踢一個街友。摩根擔心那個街友會被打死。他決定站出來為他向他們求情。

摩　　根：你可以有點慈悲嗎？他是無辜的。

布魯斯：別煩！可惡！你不應該對抗我。

摩　　根：老兄，我不必跟你解釋太多，但這樣做不對。

布魯斯：你是個魯蛇。他是沒用的東西。你無法保護他。

摩　　根：忽視生命不是勇敢，珍惜生命不是軟弱。

布魯斯：我知道你的一舉一動。笨蛋、瘦竹竿……

摩　　根：你怎麼可以再打擊我？

布魯斯：你這狡猾的狗！你讓我唱獨角戲。

摩　　根：滾，你這厭煩的、說謊的、不忠實的卑鄙小人！

單字片語解析

lousy *adj.* 厭煩的
A chatterbox is very lousy.
一個喋喋不休的人讓人厭煩。

unfaithful *adj.* 不忠實的
His unfaithful deed irritates everybody in the company.
他不忠的行為讓公司的每個人生氣。

creep *n.* 卑鄙小人
Don't make a deal with a creep.
不要跟卑鄙小人做交易。

你還可以這樣說

★ bring me lower 打擊
也可以這樣說 strike at
My enemy tries every effort to strike at me.（我的敵人努力打擊我。）

★ attack
The boxer attacks his opponent.（那拳擊手攻擊他的對手。）

★ take away from 使離開；拿開

也可以這樣說 move off

You cannot move my baby away from me.（你不能將我的寶貝拿走。）

★ get away

The prisoner got away from jail.（那犯人逃離監獄。）

生活知識小補給

　　彈力女超人的彈力能成為皮艇，她應是當前橡膠材質的超人。談到橡膠，讓我們想到橡膠樹。這邊讓我們來了解一下整棵橡膠樹對人類的貢獻：橡膠樹的汁液是天然橡膠最主要來源，廣泛地運用於工業、國防、交通、醫藥衛生領域和日常生活等方面；種子可以榨油為製造油漆和肥皂的原料；橡膠果殼可製優質纖維，作為製優質活性炭及醋酸等的化工原料；而木材則可製樹脂粘合板。真是大自然贈與的珍貴樹木呢！

1
Part

2
Part

3
Part

4
Part

Unit 12

超人特攻隊
Tear Sb. Apart

動畫經典佳句

"Exploiting every loophole, dodging every obstacle! They're penetrating the bureaucracy!"
鑽每個漏洞，躲過障礙！他們滲透所有官僚作風。

"They will pay through the nose to get it."
他們將傾家蕩產。

"It tore me apart. But I learned an important lesson. You cannot count on anyone."
我心都碎了，但我學到一個重要一課，你不能依賴任何人。

 **動畫內容敘述**

Returning home in Metroville, Symdrom immobilizes the Incredible with his energy ray, plans to kidnap Jack-Jack and intends on raising him as his own sidekick to fight the family someday. While the Parrs launch a rescue attach and find Syndrome tries to escape to his jet, Jack-Jack's own transforming superpowers start to impede Syndrome's escape. Helen rescues Jack-Jack, and Bob defeats Syndrome by throwing his own car at the jet, causing him to be sucked into the jet's turbine and killed. Three months later, the Parrs have adjusted to normal life, but when a new villain called the Undermine arrives, the family wear their superhero outfits, preparing to battle the new foe.

回到都會山家中,大壞蛋辛拉登用他的能量電流定住超人一家,他計畫綁架小傑,意圖養大他,和超人一家人對抗。這一家人發現辛拉登的逃脫計畫,準備要救小傑。小傑這時展現他變形的超能力,讓辛拉登無法得逞。海倫救小傑,鮑勃把他的車丟向飛機,造成辛拉登的風衣捲進飛機渦輪而死掉。三個月後,這一家人回歸正常生活,但一個叫採礦大師的新壞蛋出現,這一家人再度披上超人服裝,出發打擊新敵人。

(參考網站:*http://disney.wikia.com/wiki/The_Incredibles*)

1 Part

2 Part

3 Part

4 Part

 情境對話 🎧 Track 48

Kelly is a bank teller in charge of mortgage. She has a very mean supervisor, Deborah. She suggests that Kelly should only approve the mortgage to the rich. However, Kelly finds out the poor need more help than the rich. She believes that granting the mortgage is the only way to make their dreams come true. Nnetheless, Deborah doesn't think so.

Deborah: What happened? The creditors exploiting every loophole, dodging every obstacle! They're penetrating the bureaucracy!

Kelly: I did nothing at all.

Deborah: What the heck am I gonna do to you? Your dear friend told me you grant most of them.

Kelly: Really? It tore me apart. But I learned an important lesson. You cannot count on anyone. I just fulfill their dreams. The small enterprise could possibly be very successful.

Deborah: Their dreams cannot make me money. You will pay through the nose for this.

Kelly: I just perform a public service, but you act like that's bad.

▸▸ **中譯**

凱利是個銀行行員負責貸款。她有一個很邪惡的主任，黛博拉。她建議凱莉應該只貸款給有錢人。然而，凱莉發現，窮人比有錢人更需要幫助。她相信貸款給他們是唯一能讓他們美夢成真的方法。可是，黛博拉不這麼認為。

黛博拉：發生甚麼事？貸款人鑽每個漏洞，躲過障礙！他們滲透所有官僚作風。

凱　莉：我甚麼都沒做。

黛博拉：搞甚麼鬼，我要怎麼處置你？你親愛的朋友告訴我你同意大部分的貸款。

凱　莉：真的嗎？我心都碎了，但我學到重要的一課，你不能依賴任何人。我只是滿足他們的夢想。那些小企業可能會非常成功。

黛博拉：他們的夢想沒法讓我賺錢。你將為此傾家蕩產。

凱　莉：我只是做公益，但你看來就像說這是壞事。

單字片語解析

loophole *n.* 孔洞

Through the loophole, we can see the habitat of ants.

透過孔洞，我們可以看到螞蟻的棲居地。

dodge *v.* 逃避

You cannot dodge the problem.

你不能逃避問題。

bureaucracy *n.* 官僚作風

The bureaucracy should be knocked down.

官僚作風應被擊倒。

你還可以這樣說

★ tear sb. apart 撕裂；撕碎

也可以這樣說 destroy

His love has been destroyed by her indifference.（他的愛被她的冷漠撕碎。）

★ fall apart

The family has fallen apart due to poverty.（這個家庭因貧窮而分裂。）

★ make sb. sad

The boy's misdeed makes her mother sad.（那男孩的罪行撕裂媽媽的心。）

★ pay through the nose 傾家蕩產

也可以這樣説 lose a family fortune

The man indulges in gambling and loses a family fortune.

（那個人沉迷於賭博而傾家蕩產。）

★ be reduced to poverty and ruin

Due to the flood, the family is reduced to poverty and ruin.

（因為水災，這個家庭傾家蕩產了。）

★ be brought to total ruin

Addicting to drugs, Johnson is brought to total ruin.（強森因吸毒而傾家蕩產。）

生活知識小補給

　　小小一隻小鳥，與超大型飛機相撞，在一般人看來，猶如以卵擊石。然而事實卻並非如此。飛機與飛鳥在空中相撞，輕者飛機不能正常飛行；重者機毀人亡，釀成重大災難。過去重大的鳥擊事件，如：1996 年 7 月，比利時空軍的一架 Lockheed C-130 運輸機在荷蘭的 Eindhoven 機場進場時遭鳥擊，墜落在跑道上，造成 37 名乘員中有 30 名死亡，是史上傷亡最慘重的軍機鳥擊事件，所以飛機真的怕小鳥。

Learn Smart! 060

看動畫瘋美式英語！
魔鏡魔鏡，救救我的 Chinglish! (MP3)

作　　者	呂丹宜 Dannie Lu
發 行 人	周瑞德
執行總監	齊心瑀
企劃編輯	魏于婷
校　　對	編輯部
封面構成	高鍾琪

內頁構成	菩薩蠻數位文化有限公司
印　　製	大亞彩色印刷製版股份有限公司
初　　版	2016 年 7 月
定　　價	新台幣 379 元
出　　版	倍斯特出版事業有限公司
電　　話	(02) 2351-2007
傳　　真	(02) 2351-0887
地　　址	100 台北市中正區福州街 1 號 10 樓之 2
E-mail	best.books.service@gmail.com
網　　址	www.bestbookstw.com

港澳地區總經銷	泛華發行代理有限公司
地　　址	香港新界將軍澳工業邨駿昌街 7 號 2 樓
電　　話	(852) 2798-2323
傳　　真	(852) 2796-5471

國家圖書館出版品預行編目資料

看動畫瘋美式英語!魔鏡魔鏡,救救我的
Chinglish! / 呂丹宜著. -- 初版. -- 臺北
市 : 倍斯特, 2016.07
　面 ; 　公分. -- (Learn smart! ; 60)
ISBN 978-986-92855-3-7(平裝附光碟片)

1.英語 2.讀本

　　805.18　　　105010396